Yogi and Johan
The Beginnings

Mysore N. Prakash Ph.D.

Published by
Dharma Vision LLC
www.dharmavision.com

ISBN: 978-0-9818237-2-0

Yogi and Johan, The Beginnings
by Mysore N. Prakash Ph.D.

Editors: Rohith Prakash, and Robert C. Wigton, J.D., Ph.D.

Library of Congress Control Number: 2011932775

This is a work of fiction. All of the characters, names, incidents, organizations, and dialogue are either the products of the author's imagination or are used fictitiously.

Printed in the United States of America

Table of Contents

Prologue

I looked at my watch and saw that it was already 7:00 PM. My American Airlines flight from New Delhi to Chicago was scheduled to depart just after midnight. I still had more than five hours before the flight and felt calm since all my packing was already done. The concierge had booked my cab at 9:30 PM, and she had assured me that the cabby would take me to the airport in 40 minutes, giving me plenty of time to go through the departure formalities. I went down to the restaurant and had a quick dinner. As soon as I was done with my dinner, I walked to the front desk to clear my account. The clerk greeted me with a friendly smile and asked me how my stay had been. Everyone at the Taj had been very friendly, and I was extremely pleased with their service.

"Everything was delightful. Nothing to complain about," I replied enthusiastically.

I gave her my American Express card and waited for her to print my final statement. As she handed back my card with the statement and asked me to sign on the dotted line, she asked me a question I often get asked in India.

"Dr. Prakash, are you from the city of Mysore?"

She was obviously curious about my name. My first name, Mysore, also happens to be a city in southern India. Before I answered her question, I looked into her eyes to see if I could guess her regional background. I could not really guess - she could have been from any of the thirty or so Indian states.

"Yes, I grew up in Mysore. However, for the past thirty years or so I have been living in the United States," I replied.

"That is very interesting. I have an uncle in Mysore, and my family is from a village called Beerur near Mysore," she replied with a sense of excitement. Her excitement was like that of a person who had just found a lost relative or a friend.

"That is fascinating. Wherever I go in India, I often meet someone with a connection to Mysore. Isn't it a small world?" I replied as I took back my card and the statement and bid her goodbye.

I was not in the mood to waste any more time at the hotel. I was anxious to go to the airport on time. I was nervous about the infamous Delhi traffic jams and was not willing to relax until I had completed my check-in at the airport.

I had come to India from Dallas four weeks prior for a business project. One of my clients, a large wireless operator, was looking at several options to expand their network. They needed a business expert to evaluate their options and give them a recommendation on the optimal way to expand their business. They had approached my company as we specialized in such projects. My company had selected me to run the project. I was more than eager to take up the project as it gave me a chance to visit my dad who lives in the southern city of Bangalore. Indeed, I had gone twice during my stay to visit my dad, which had been quite a treat for both of us.

The project had gone very well. I had met marketing, engineering, and business teams from my client's company, and together we had worked day and night to develop several options for network and business expansion. I had crunched and re-crunched the numbers and had finally developed three recommendations that we presented to the executive team. That was just two days ago. They had liked all three options and had a tough time settling on one of them. In the end, they politely thanked me for my work and told me that they would make the final choice over the next week or so. I was not bothered by that as I was confident that whichever plan they chose, they would have a successful result. With my work done, I was ready to leave Delhi and eager to re-join my family in Dallas.

I walked out of the hotel towards the cab that was waiting for me. The bell boy had already loaded my luggage and all that was left for me was to thank him with a nice tip. As soon as I got into my cab, the cab driver zipped out of the hotel weaving through the notorious Delhi traffic speeding towards Indira Gandhi International Airport. I was amazed at his skill as he managed to change from lane to lane to keep our car moving. Right at that point, I noticed that there was a long traffic jam ahead of us. I also noticed that there was some large scale construction in the vicinity.

"Don't worry, Sir, I know a way to get around this mess. You will be at the airport in no time," my driver assured me.

He then went over the curb, started going down the side of the highway, and entered a small road that led us into a congested neighborhood. In no time, he was zipping through the area making swift turns while continuously honking. I closed my eyes and started meditating just to keep my nerves calm.

When I finally opened my eyes, my driver had indeed avoided the traffic jam and was back on the highway. The rest of the drive was uneventful, and we were in front of the airport at 10:10 PM. Just as the concierge had assured me, the driver had brought me to the airport in exactly 40 minutes.

I paid my driver as he put my luggage in a cart and helped me get onto a ramp that led to a crowded hall. I went though the first level of security screening where the officer made sure that I was a bona-fide traveler with a valid ticket. After going through security, I got my boarding pass, checked in my luggage, and went through immigration. Finally, I was in the departure lounge with just my laptop in a leather case. I looked at the boarding pass to see that my seat number was 14B, an aisle seat.

I felt greatly relieved and extremely relaxed. I looked around to see if I could get some coffee, and started walking towards a coffee shop that was in the lounge area.

"Can I help you, Sir? We have several varieties of tea. Perhaps you would like to try our spiced tea?" the attendant gave me his pitch, making me change my mind about coffee.

"Spiced tea sounds good. I will have a cup," I replied. The attendant gave me a big smile approving my selection, and added a little bonus for me.

"I am going to add some extra spices for you, Sir. You are really going to like this tea," he guaranteed as he took out a plastic bag and added some dark colored material which looked like some sort of dried leaves. I gave him a fifty rupee bill for the tea and walked back to the sitting area. I sat down, completely relaxed, and started sipping my tea.

The tea had a sweetish taste. Yet the spices were subtle and had a soothing effect on me. It felt so soothing that it almost made me sleepy.

At that time, a tall skinny young man wearing torn jeans and a T-shirt with a backpack sat in a seat that was three rows in front of me. He had brownish, wavy hair and looked around six feet tall. His T-shirt had the logo of the Indian Wells tennis tournament. I assumed that he was probably an American from California who was visiting India as a tourist.

I went back to savoring my tea. It seemed like I had never had a cup of tea that tasted so good. I looked up again and stared at the young tourist. He had now settled down and had closed his eyes. He looked like he was sleeping; his legs were crossed in the lotus position. I realized that he was actually meditating. That really got my attention.

The young tourist looked like he was around nineteen or twenty years in age. Up to this point, my trip to India had been normal. I knew instantly that it was not going to be normal any more.

When I looked up again at the young tourist, I was startled that he was not actually sitting on his seat; he appeared to be levitating and I tried to rub my eyes to make sure that I was not hallucinating. I wondered if the *teawala*[1] had put some strange substance in my tea. What was that dark powder the attendant added to my tea? Was it *bhang* or *hashish*[2]? Myriads of questions went through my head as I looked around to see if any of the other passengers in the lounge area had noticed this young man levitating. It seemed like everyone else was oblivious to what was going on and went about their business in a casual way. Surely, something wasn't right here, I concluded.

"It's all right Dr. Prakash. Please come and sit in front of me," I heard a voice, whisper. From the American accent, I immediately knew it was from that young tourist. The voice frightened me as it was not coming from outside, but rather

---

1   *Tea vendor.*

2   *Bhang and Hashish are derived from leaves or flowers of Indian Cannabis.*

originating in my own head. How did he do that? Even more frightening was how he knew my name? Reluctantly, I moved to a seat in front of the young man. "Do you want me to call you Satya? I know you have used the pen name Satya Avatar," the voice added.

The whole thing was incredible to me. I had indeed published a novel The Courtesan and the Sadhu under my pen name Satya Avatar. But how was it possible that someone I had never met in my life could be aware of my name and my background? It made me nervous, frightened, and confused. Nevertheless, I garnered some strength and replied.

"It is true I have used the name Satya Avatar, but you can just call me Mysore," I whispered.

"No need to talk, Mysore. I can read your thoughts. Let's just communicate telepathically," the young man replied still levitating.

"That is fine with me," I replied in thoughts, trying to be brave.

"You are probably wondering who I am, Mysore. Let me give you some information about my background. My name is Johan. I was actually born and raised in Plano, Texas. I came to India last year to meet a yogi in the Himalayas. He is not just any yogi – he is known as Maha yogi. He has accepted me as his student; and I am on my way to be a yogi too," Johan explained.

I felt a little better as I was from Plano as well, a northern suburb of Dallas, which was where I was heading. I started believing in Johan's power to communicate through telepathy.

Nevertheless, my education and religious upbringing got in the way. As someone who had completed a doctorate degree in engineering, I had always considered myself to be rational. I was skeptical of the existence of supernatural powers yogic or otherwise. Perhaps it was the result of my religious upbringing. My mother was a strict adherent to the *Advaita*[3] tradition and had never accepted the existence of supernatural powers. Indeed, she was extremely suspicious of all people claiming to have supernatural powers. In her belief system, only God, the controller of *Māya*,[4] possessed powers beyond the laws of nature. Anyone else who claimed such powers was an illusionist at best. On the other hand, my father was more open-minded. Although he had spent most of his life as a mathematician, he believed that there were many aspects of scientific knowledge that were still to be uncovered, and as such science was currently unable to explain many supernatural phenomenon. This, perhaps, stemmed from the fact that as a teenager, my father himself had witnessed a supernatural event for which he had never found a scientific explanation.

Coming back to the present, my thoughts took me back to the cup of tea I had just consumed. Perhaps due to my maternal influence, I was now convinced that this whole thing was some sort of delusional effect of whatever drug was in the tea.

"Do not be silly, Mysore. There was no drug whatsoever in your tea," Johan said, answering my question.

"What is it that you want from me, Johan? Why have you possessed me? You aren't going to hurt me, right?" I had to ask him as I was now scared. To be honest, I have never been tolerant of physical pain.

"I am in no way going to hurt you, Mysore. Yogis never hurt anyone. I have come to you because I want you to chronicle my journey, about how I came to meet my guru,

---

3   *Advaita tradition is one of the branches of Hindu theology.*

4   *Māya is the Divine energy or force that drives the material world.*

and how he taught me the yogic powers." He paused for a few seconds and continued, "Let us go to the gate now. They are going to announce our flight."

Johan then opened his eyes and got up. He gave me a faint smile as we started walking towards the gate. I could hear the attendant announcing details of our flight as we walked towards the agent who was standing near a podium ready to collect boarding passes.

"We will be seated next to each other, and I will tell you my story during the journey," Johan explained as we walked towards the business class cabin. I looked at my boarding pass and saw my seat number slowly change from 14B to 12A. How my seat number went through that transformation right in front of my eyes was a mystery to me. But this was the least of my worries, and I did not bother thinking about it too much.

When we were settled down in our seats, Johan in 12 B and I in 12A, a flight attendant came to offer us some juices. However, when I turned towards Johan he was in deep meditation again. I put on the headset and started listening to the channel that was carrying some classic rock songs. I soon dozed off and was only woken by the noise of the flight attendants serving dinner.

I was not very hungry and decided to eat lightly. I noticed that Johan was still meditating. After the dinner was over and the flight attendants had cleared all the aisles and turned off the lights, I sat in my seat listening to music wondering when Johan would start telling me his story.

During the last sixty minutes or so since I had met this young American yogi, I had experienced a confluence of emotions. First, I was scared, even fearing that he would do me some harm. As I realized that I was not in any danger whatsoever, I became skeptical, skeptical that the levitation

I had witnessed was some sort of an optical illusion and that the voices in my head were caused by some chemical imbalance in my head. However, how had my seat number change from 14B to 12A right in front of my eyes? There had to be an explanation for all this beyond linear logic. It had to be beyond the known frontiers of science. I suddenly felt a surge of excitement and was now eager to hear Johan's story, so much that I was now getting restless and started rapidly tapping the back of my palm with my fingers. It was as if I were trying to send my own signals to the young yogi.

A few minutes later, the music stopped, and I could hear Johan's voice coming clearly through the channel.

"I will now start telling you my story, Mysore. Please pay attention to all the details. I want to make sure that you chronicle the events accurately. Also, I want you to write my story using your real name." Johan's voice was clear, and his instructions were specific. I turned to see what he was doing, and, not surprisingly, I found him meditating with his eyes closed.

Over the next several hours, Johan narrated his incredible life story. By the time we reached Chicago, the story that he had narrated had not been completed. He told me that there was more to come and that he would get in touch with me later to give the details. When I offered to give him my contact information, he assured me that it was not necessary.

When we got out of the plane in Chicago, he was on his way to San Francisco whereas I was on my way to Dallas. He smiled at me and vanished right in front of my eyes. It happened so fast that it felt like the rest of the airport had frozen in time and he was zipping through the lines as no one was even trying to stop him or check his papers. Having experienced his powers first hand, I was not surprised by what I saw. That was the last time I saw Johan. However, as he had promised, he continued to get in touch with me through telepathy to update his story and his whereabouts. What follows is the story that Johan narrated to me. It is the story of a young American yogi. This is the story of Yogi and Johan.

CHAPTER 1
Texas

It was an early September evening in North Texas; the sky was clear, and the air was warm. Johan stepped out of his house and decided to take a short walk to relax. He was anxious as he was leaving Plano the next day on his way to California to start his collegiate life. No doubt college life was something to look forward to but at the same time, he was a little nervous as this was the first time he was going to be on his own. As he walked out of his house, he called out to tell his dad that he was going to be gone for a while, but he was not certain that his dad heard him; he made sure that he locked the house and started walking away. As he picked up his pace, he slowly slid his hands into the pockets of his shorts and his fingers ran into the car keys, which gave him an idea to go for a joy ride. This was something he did occasionally; he went on long drives into the rural part of Collin County east of Plano whenever he wanted to be on his own. *Well, this is the last time I will be doing this in 2007*; he mused as he got back home, went into the garage, and started his car. He backed into the alley and closed the electric garage door with his remote, and soon he was on Parker Road driving towards the eastern part of Collin County.

He had driven almost half an hour when he realized that he was now on a deserted rural road with no signs of any traffic, or for that matter, any life except for a few cows grazing the farms. As he drove further into the countryside, he could see the sun disappearing into the horizon in the rear view mirror. Within a few minutes, even the twilight would be gone and night was going to blanket the wide, open rural landscape. Suddenly, the car started sputtering and without any warning, it came to a complete halt. He looked at the dashboard for hints, it occurred to him right way that he was in trouble as the fuel gauge indicated that his tank was empty. He got out and pushed the car to the right shoulder, and looked around to see how he could get some help. Should he stay there waiting for someone to drive by so that he could tag the driver for help, or should he just walk to a nearby gas station to get some gas? As he looked around, he saw a trail that ran into a wooded area surrounding a creek nearby. A closer look revealed that the trail led into an intersection of two roads not far away and he could even see a bright light that seemed to indicate a gas station at the crossing. Johan decided to walk along the trail and brought the gas can that was in the trunk. He took the plastic can out and started walking briskly towards the intersection. Along the way he wondered if it was a bad decision to drive that evening. *I should have just stuck with my original plan*, he lamented. As he came to the creek, he noticed that there were a couple of long logs neatly placed over the ravine for hikers like him to cross the creek. He carefully walked over the logs taking care not to fall into the creek. Once he was on the other side of the creek, something eerie happened. Everything seemed to change all of a sudden; like changing the background of a computer screen. It was as if he was in a foreign land that was strange yet very familiar. Johan got a little nervous and started walking gingerly lest some unfortunate accident should happen. Suddenly, he heard someone calling him.

"Pst, come here, Johan," he heard someone calling him almost like a whisper. He stopped and looked around, and to his dismay, all he could sense was an eerie silence. He was about to continue with his journey when he heard the same voice.

"Come here Johan. I am behind the tree." The voice was louder and was much clearer this time. He also realized that it was a very familiar voice. Nevertheless, he was worried that someone dangerous could be behind the tree. He gingerly walked towards the tree when a short man holding a gun walked out from behind the tree.

Johan was astonished to see the man as he recognized him. He had no idea how he had run into him. He was, after all, a celebrity in his own right. The man handed the gun to him, and commanded.

"It is your turn to hunt today. Take the gun and start looking for that rascal rabbit."

"Why should I do that, Elmer?" Johan protested. Wasn't it always Elmer Fudd's job to chase Bugs Bunny[5]? Moreover, Johan detested hunting, perhaps, due to his mother's influence. She had preached to him enough about non-violence ever since he was a toddler.

"Don't you know today is Labor Day. It is my day off. It is your turn to chase Bugs," Elmer was firm.

Johan took the gun and stood there wondering what exactly was going on.

"You're in cartoon land, Johan. Look there, far away, at that hole. That is where Bugs is hiding. I want you to go vewwwy, vewwwy slowly and smoke him out," ordered Elmer.

---

5   *Elmer Fudd and Bugs Bunny are characters in* Looney Tunes *owned and produced by Warner Bros Entertainment Inc.*

Seeing that he had no other choice, he went very slowly towards the hole making sure that he made absolutely no noise. As he got near the hole, he was astonished at what he saw; there was a neat little studio apartment inside the hole with a little bed and a fancy kitchen. However, the whole room was empty and there was no sign of Bugs anywhere. He peaked inside to make sure that the rabbit was not hiding behind the bed. Once convinced about that he got up shrugged his shoulders and scratched his head about his next step. Suddenly he heard the noise of a propeller plane that got louder by the second and before he knew, it was too close to his eardrums. Scared, he dove and fell flat on the ground to save his life and as he carefully looked up, there it was. It was a propeller plane flown by none other than Bugs Bunny himself. Smiling Bugs was looking back at him and he seemed to be saying, "What's up, doc?"

Johan was glad that he was unhurt and got up and started to think about how he was going to get out of that Looney place. Right at that time, he saw a herd of cartoon characters running towards him. There was Sylvester the cat, Daffy Duck, the Tweety Bird, Yosemite Sam, and a host of others.[6] As they ran past him, they all shouted in unison.

"Run for your life, Johan. They are going to drop the E-bomb."

"What is an E-bomb?" Johan yelled back.

"It is the *Eraser*. We'll be history," shouted back Sylvester the cat.

Johan looked up and realized that there was a giant eraser ready to erase him off cartoon land. He dropped his gun and started running as fast as he could. He was sweating

---

6 *Sylvester, Daffy Duck, Tweety and Yosemite Sam are characters in* Looney Tunes *owned and produced by Warner Bros Entertainment Inc.*

⋙ 4 ⋘

profusely and could not run anymore when suddenly he fell down with a loud thud.

Johan woke up from his dream and realized that the big thud he heard was the sound of the book he had kept on his chest hitting the floor. It was some old book about time travel. He looked at the clock and realized that it was past midnight. It was not the first time he had a dream where he had found himself in a cartoon land. He wondered why he kept having these recurring dreams about cartoon land. It was silly and ridiculous, he thought. On the other hand, maybe there was some significance. He thought that he should ask his friend Nick as he was going to major in Psychology. There must be some explanation – the gun probably represented the Iraq war he had blocked from his mind. If Nick had no answers, maybe it was time for him to seek some professional help. Perhaps, it had no significance whatsoever. He tried to forget about the dream so that he could focus on his immediate tasks. He only had two more days before he was off to California to enter Stanford.

Indeed, Johan was extremely excited to be going to Stanford. Who would not be excited to enter a prestigious institution like Stanford? Johan was a bright student with superb academic record. In addition, until two years ago, he was considered a tennis prodigy. Of course, he had not played tennis for a while now. Nevertheless, many college coaches wanted to recruit him and had offered enticing scholarships, but he was in no mood to play tennis again. He had wondered if he could have afforded to go to Stanford without tennis scholarship. His dad, however, had advised him not to worry about the college expenses, and he had accepted admission as a regular candidate.

A few years ago, he was considered a bright prospect to become a professional player at a very young age. Unfortunately, it was a promise that was never fulfilled. Things had taken an unexpected detour in his tennis career. He sighed as he did not want to think about that too much.

Johan had shown tremendous talent in hitting the tennis ball as he progressed in competitive tennis. While he struggled with focus in his very early years, he had soon developed tremendous tennis skills which had propelled him to the elite echelon of junior tennis players in Texas. Even before he became a highly ranked tennis player, his strokes were natural, and it was like he needed no coaching at all. However, whenever he tried to play in the tournaments, something unexplained would happen, and his game would collapse. This had frustrated his mother beyond reason. However, only Johan knew the reason, and he kept it to himself. There were those recurring visions which were often scary yet they captivated him. For some unexplained reason he had decided to keep it as his own secret and had never told anyone about them, including his mom or dad. Then there was the yogi who was at the center of a second set of visions who had become his long distance coach and mentor which had dramatically changed his tennis career.

Johan sat on the floor next to his bed in the lotus position. He closed his eyes and started meditating. As he immersed himself in a deep meditative state, he tried to send telepathic signals to contact the yogi. It was like trying to send signals into outer space with no response whatsoever. He tried harder and harder to connect to the yogi. The results were the same, like the last thousand times or so. He felt drained and exhausted. He started perspiring profusely and collapsed. He felt empty, and when he opened his eyes, he felt tears coming out. *How am I going to fill this void*, he silently cried.

It was during one of his tennis tournaments that he had first met Nick Hamilton. Nick was another talented tennis player he had played against since he was nine. They were in the same age group competing in the same tournaments. Their first match was in Tyler just one hundred miles or so from Dallas. Although Johan won the match, it was not an easy victory. They were very close to each other in ranking for several years. However, once the yogi took an interest in his tennis, Johan's game took such a quantum jump that Nick's game was no longer a match for him.

The familiarity and occasional get-together during tournaments slowly blossomed into a friendship between Johan and Nick. Over time, as they came to know each other better, they realized that they had several common interests beyond tennis. They both liked reading about history, and they were both interested in world affairs. Of course, they both closely followed the professional circuit, and Federer was their hero. While Johan was the more serious type, Nick was the jovial one who could crack a joke on any topic and at any time. Nick had applied for Stanford as well, and Johan was extremely happy when he found out that Nick had gotten a positive nod. They had decided to be roommates in the dorm, and both were looking forward to the challenge and excitement.

Johan started packing his belongings into a big suitcase he was going to check. As he emptied his closet and packed them into the suitcase, he realized that he did not have a lot to take with him. There was some space left for him to pack his books. He had read many novels over the years. Some were science fiction and others were books on fantasy. He loved fantasy stories, and maybe that was the reason why he kept having recurring cartoon-land dreams, he mused. There was a book called "Pancha Tantra", which literally meant five principles. He had bought that book in Europe when he was in Holland several years ago. He liked the ancient stories of Pancha Tantra, and often made his own extensions of the stories with elements of science fiction. He even thought about writing a modern version of Pancha Tantra sometime.

As he packed the book in his suitcase, he thought about his mother. He tried to control his tears as he tried to suppress his emotions. He wished that there were someway he could contact her. He wanted to hear her voice, but at this point, he was willing to settle for a simple instant message. He glanced over his list of contacts on his IM list and was disappointed to see that "mom" was not highlighted. Why did she have to disappear from his life like that? It was simply not fair.

The next day he and his dad did the last minute shopping. They went to the Wal-Mart on US 75 and bought everything he needed for the first month in the dorm. He also bought some crackers and nuts in case he needed some snacks. John was proud of his son, proud of the fact that Johan was going to a prestigious school. However, he still wished that Johan had selected Texas A&M, his alma mater. That way he could visit Johan whenever he wished since it was just two hundred miles from Dallas to College Station.

"You really want to go to California, Johan?" John asked half jokingly as they came out of Wal-Mart.

Johan did not say anything as he knew that his dad was not really serious. Nevertheless, he also knew that they were going to miss each other and the separation was not going to be easy.

"Will you be visiting me often, Dad?" John said instinctively.

"Send me an IM and I will be in California in a few hours."

"In a few hours?" Johan did not suppress his surprise.

"Yes, I have decided to lease a private plane."

Johan was not sure what to say. Of course, John was a licensed pilot. He had, however, never mentioned the desire to own a plane. He looked away from his dad and stared at the holiday traffic on US 75. He was a little too overwhelmed to say anything.

Johan knew that his dad was very lonely. He was lonely too. Things had become topsy-turvy in their lives over the last two years. Four years ago, his was a picture perfect family. He had his loving parents. His dad's business was picking up nicely thanks to rising oil prices. His mom was happy with his school work, and his grades were exactly where he wanted them to be. His tennis career had reached a point where they had to make a decision about Johan's commitment to tennis as a professional career. However, all that had changed one day without even a trace of warning. His mom, Nicole, had disappeared from their lives without leaving any clues about what had happened to her. There was a frantic search for her. They had even hired a private detective. All they could trace was that she had flown from Dallas to London, and after that no one knew anything about her whereabouts.

"Can you do that, Dad? What about your business?" Johan asked.

"I am actually thinking of winding down my business, Johan. I am even thinking of doing something different maybe in California itself."

"That will be cool. You can visit me as often as you like," Johan sounded excited.

Just then, his phone rang. It was Nick, and he walked away from the car as he started talking to his friend. After a while, he came back to their car and got inside.

"It was Nick. He wanted to know when we were going to be at the airport tomorrow. He is going to be on the same flight, Dad," Johan informed his dad as he closed the car door.

"He is flying commercial? I thought his whole family was flying in their private jet." John was a little surprised that Nick, who came from a wealthy family, was flying commercial.

"Well, that was their original plan. They changed that plan since his grandpa got airsick a month ago when they all flew in their jet," Johan explained.

"You never told me about it. So, his grandpa is flying with them?"

"Sorry Dad, I forgot to tell you that. Yeah, both his grandpa and grandma will fly with them," Johan explained.

That evening Johan spent the whole time finishing his packing. When he was finally done, he turned his laptop on, and started listening to some music. It was first the Doors, and then it was AC/DC. Classic rock had become his favorite music. He liked the Bad Company, Rolling Stones, and the Beatles too. AC/DC was another favorite group of his; perhaps, that had something to do with Federer his Tennis hero. As he was listening to the music, an IM window popped. There was a moment of hopeless anticipation, almost a desperate wish. He hoped that it was his mom.

"*All set for tomorrow*" was the message in the IM window. It was Nick.

"*Yup, how about you?*" replied Johan.

"*All set. I can't wait for tomorrow.*"

"*What're you doing?*"

"*Reading a book on Psychology and listening to Stealers Wheel.*"

"*Stuck in the middle with you?*"

"*Yeah.*"

"*Oh, I had my Looney Tunes dream again,*" Johan added.

"*You have them every time there is something important the next day.*"

"*Yeah.*"

"*It has something to do with your connection to that yogi. Remember how it started right after you lost connection with him,*" Nick replied.

"*Yeah. I don't want to think about it though. I'm too tired.*"

"*Good night. See you at the airport.*"

"*OK. See you at the airport.*"

When he was about to go to sleep, he heard a knock on door. It was his dad holding a hanger with some sort of covered garment in his hand.

"I have a gift for you," announced John as he entered Johan's room.

"What is it, Dad?"

"It's a suit for you. I thought that you should have a nice one to attend important events," replied John as he took the plastic cover off. Johan looked at the dark blue woolen suit. It looked very expensive and wondered why his father had spent so much money on it.

"Where did you buy it?"

"Never mind where I bought it. I thought it looked good on you. I remember Nicole saying that you looked best in dark blue suits," replied John.

Johan took the suit, gave it another close look, and hugged his dad. They stayed like that for a while as they were both lost thinking about Nicole.

The next morning, Johan was up before dawn. He had shaved and showered even before his dad had gotten up. He kept his luggage and the tennis bag in the SUV and went to the kitchen to have breakfast. He decided to make some pancakes as he was very hungry. As he was about to place his plate on the kitchen table, his dad came down from his room.

"Do you want some pancakes?" asked Johan.

"Sure, just a couple," replied John.

Johan looked at his dad and realized that he was tired. He wondered about that. Was moving to California taking a mental toll on him? Was it separation anxiety? Of course, his dad was coming with him to Stanford and staying in the area for a couple of days. During that time, he had arranged for one of his assistants to handle his business.

Johan had always assumed that his dad was a strong man until that night they both realized that Johan's mother was missing forever. They had concluded that they may never see her again. John knew about the hidden demons that had tormented Nicole for a long time. He had kept it a secret and shielded Johan all his life. John was terribly sad, and he had finally let Johan know the truth about his mother. That night was something that Johan had been trying to forget. He did not want to think about it anymore, and he had tried his best to erase it altogether from his memory. He had meditated endlessly, tried yoga for hours at a time. It had calmed him down, subdued his pain, but he was never the same again. He had repeatedly called out for the yogi hoping that he could get him out of his emotional hell. Unfortunately for Johan, he had lost the connection to the yogi when he needed him most.

"You are really eager to leave Plano, Johan."

"Not eager to leave you dad. I am eager to go to Stanford," Johan clarified.

"Can we leave at 10:00 AM?" Johan was eager.

"But your flight is at 12:30 PM. It is just a thirty to forty minutes drive," John replied.

"Dad, please. I am nervous. I want to be at the airport as soon as we can."

The next few hours seemed like an eternity to Johan. He helped his dad put his bag in the back of the SUV. Finally, when they got into the SUV and started driving towards the airport, he felt relieved. They were soon on the turnpike. As they drove on the turnpike, random thoughts kept creeping in Johan's mind. First it was the name of the turnpike. Some local politician had convinced the suburbs to name it George H. W. Bush turnpike. Some were not pleased as happens with everything in America. Someone even called it the highway that went from nowhere to nowhere, just like the Bush policy. Johan thought that it was unfair. The highway did provide an easy access to people from Plano traveling to the "Big" airport. His dad was not thrilled with that analogy either; he had liked George H. W. Bush.

They were soon inside the DFW airport. They parked their vehicle in long term parking and took the shuttle to the terminal.

After checking the luggage, they went inside the terminal through the security check point. They reached their gate and waited for Nick and his family to join them.

Chapter 2

John's Tragedy

John Watt was born in the West Texas town of Lubbock. He was the only child in his family. It was like his family always had a one child policy; his dad and his grandfather were also only children. John's ancestors were originally from Scotland and had migrated to Texas several generations ago. John did not have much of an extended family as he had no aunts or uncles; not even a great uncle or great aunt. His extended families were the other kids he knew in his school. After he had graduated from high school, he had enrolled at Texas A&M University with the intention of becoming a petroleum engineer. Of course, West Texas was famous for the oil industry and his intention was to start his own business related to oil and gas once he graduated from college. Things were going very well during his first year at the college. He had gotten good grades, and after spending first few weeks of summer at home, he had come back to College Station for a summer job. It was a job he had gotten in the Geo-Physics department helping a professor analyze seismic data collected from field surveys. The seismic data was based on a series of measurements collected from large geographical areas that had shown potential for oil fields, and the professor was developing what he called "next generation" algorithms to pin point the location of oil wells.

Things were going very well that summer, and John had nothing to complain about as he received a handsome stipend for his work but all that suddenly changed one day. It was late summer and he was in a pizza parlor near the campus enjoying his dinner with some of his friends from the lab where he worked. They were excited about the coming fall semester especially about their football team's prospects the next season. While John was in the middle of some enthused discussions about the possibility of winning the national championship, his roommate had entered the parlor with a grim look on his face. John looked at his roommate and something in his eyes told him that his friend had brought him some terrible news. His friend, Mike, signaled John to step out of the parlor and as they quietly walked out, his room mate who was visibly upset began to brief John.

"John, I had a phone call just a few minutes ago. I came here as fast as I could," Mike hesitated for a moment, not knowing what to say.

"What phone call, Mike? What are you talking about," John was confused.

"It was from Lubbock. It was someone who lives near your parents' house."

John had a chill in his whole body. It was as if he knew what he was going to hear next.

"It seems that there was a sudden storm in the Lubbock area. After the storm subsided, someone saw a car floating in a creek. It was that of your parents," Mike relayed what he had heard on the phone. He looked into John's eyes and saw that he was in tears; his whole body had frozen.

"I am sorry, John. Whoever saw the accident did their best to save your parents, but it was too late," Mike explained.

John could picture the whole event now. There was a sudden torrential rain in West Texas that morning and the storm had come so unexpectedly that John's parents who were returning from their weekly grocery shopping were caught in the rain. They tried to reach their home as quickly as they could but the rain was falling so hard that they could hardly see the road they were on. The entire vicinity was like a muddy lake, and it felt like several inches of rain were pouring down every minute. They had never seen a storm like that in their entire lives. In their rush to get home they were crossing a bridge over a swollen creek, and a wall of water that was almost six feet high had swept their car into the creek.

The news was a terrible blow to John, and he collapsed, crying uncontrollably. He did not know what to do or how to cope with the horrific news. The next thing John remembered was that he had passed out. When he woke up, he realized that he was back in his room and his friends were waiting for him to come out of his unconscious state.

When John finally awoke, Mike offered to drive him back to Lubbock and John accepted as he was in no state to drive at that moment. He was too upset and shaken. At the same time, he knew that he had the responsibility to do the proper last rites for his parents, and he wanted to make sure the proper funeral arrangements were made. John was not very religious; nevertheless, he wanted to do their funeral the right way as his parents were traditional and had attended the same congregation all their lives.

Mike stayed with him the whole time. It was undoubtedly the most difficult time in John's young life. His neighbors helped him with the funeral arrangements, and when it was all over, Mike wanted to go back to College Station as he could not afford to stay away from his summer job any longer. John agreed with his decision, and thanked him for all the support he had given. John was now all alone in the house and felt like he was trapped. What haunted him were not ghosts or spirits but memories of his childhood days with his parents. The next day, he got up late in the morning and stayed on the living room sofa almost like a zombie wondering what he was going to do. He felt like a ship without a rudder. Right at that moment, he heard the bell ring. He slowly got up, went to the front door, and saw two men waiting outside. One of them was Mr. Thomson, an insurance agent that John knew pretty well as Mr. Thomson was close to his parents. He, however, was not familiar with the other gentleman and John opened the door and let the two men come inside the house.

"This is Mr. Forrester, John. I am sorry that we have to come and disturb your solitary moment," Mr. Thompson introduced the other gentlemen.

"Hello, John. I am an attorney, and I am the executor of your parent's will. I wanted to inform you about what is in the will," Mr. Forrester announced, introducing himself.

John signaled the two men to sit on the sofa as he sat down on the chair next to them.

"The gist of the will is this, John. Your parents had a life insurance from my company. There is almost $50K in that. In addition, they had a small nest egg of $15K in stocks and bonds. All that goes to you according to their instructions," explained Mr. Thompson.

Sixty five thousand is a lot of money but that was no replacement for his parents. He stared at the two gentlemen for a while as no one spoke any further. Then he looked up at the ceiling and wondered about the house. How much mortgage is left on this house, he wondered. As if he had read John's mind, Mr. Thompson continued.

"Well, you need to decide on the house. Do you want to sell it or do you want to rent it when you are in college?"

John did not know what to say. He was not a financial wizard, but he knew that managing a rental house from College Station was not going to be easy.

"I think I will sell the house and pay off the mortgage. I want to give all the furniture to some charity. I cannot bear to stay here any more," John replied softly.

"That is probably a wise decision. You may have another $25-35K in equity in the house," replied the lawyer knowing very well John was immensely hurt.

John, authorized the lawyer to put the house on sale, and signed all the required papers. Within two weeks the house was sold, and all the household goods in the house were given to charity. When it was all said and done, there was nearly $100K in John's account, a lot of money in 1981. John knew that he was financially secure now; however, it meant nothing to him at that point. What was the meaning of financial security without any emotional security? Moreover, he was in no mental condition to make right decisions about his money. Fortunately, for him, Mr. Thompson was a trusted adviser. He advised him to put 50% of the money in blue chip stocks, 30% in bonds, and the rest in cash. He even took him to an established brokerage company and helped him set up an account.

"You know, John, the interest rates are high now, and the market has tanked. Do not worry about that. The rates are bound to come down within few years and the markets will soar. Meanwhile, you will get a handsome dividend from your stocks. By the time you graduate, you may be a rich man," was Mr. Thompson's advice.

With all his financial affairs now settled, John was ready to go back to College Station and begin his sophomore year.

However, the more he thought about that, the more he was now confused. He was not sure how he would handle his studies as he now had fundamental questions about life and its purpose. He wanted to be left alone and not bothered by any of the day to day routines – even college routines. He paced up and down the house wondering about his next move and finally, he decided to do something very radical. The first thought that came to him was to go to a far off place like Bolivia or Nepal and join other fellow American tourists and just explore life. He closed his eyes and tried to visualize his life as a hippie in a foreign land. That did not appeal to him very much. He finally decided to discontinue his college and take a break for a year or so to discover his real passion. He would drive to Dallas and work until his mind was clear enough to make an intelligent decision. He did not know what type of job he could get as a college drop out. He was going to have to do some serious thinking on the way to Dallas.

He packed his clothes, books, and a few other belongings and he made sure that he had his important papers with him. He took his bags, dumped them into his parents' car, and slowly got in to the car. It was a few years old, but was still in good condition as his dad had maintained it well. He felt sad as it was time for him to bid good bye to his childhood home, but he knew he had to move on. Soon, he was driving along US 84. In less than two hours, he had merged into the I-20 traffic and was cruising towards Dallas. As he approached Abilene, he saw a squadron of Air Force planes flying in the distant sky and it appeared like they were in some sort of flight routine. The more he observed them the more he had a strange feeling inside his head. It was as if some strange muffled voice was trying to tell him something. Suddenly, the voice got clearer and he could hear the voice telling him to join the air force. Soon, the voice was getting louder and louder inside his head like it was commanding him to join the Air Force.

John halted at a trucker's stop, filled his car with gas, and went into the large diner that was next to the gas station. He asked the girl at the counter if she had a Dallas phone book. The girl promptly took out a large phone book but advised him that the book was probably out of date as she gave it to him. John did not mind as he only wanted the location of the US Air Force recruitment office in the Dallas area. As he expected, there were many such recruitment offices near Dallas but the one that caught his eyes was the office located in Arlington close to I-20. He decided to stop there and enquire about enlisting in the US Air Force. He knew that the USAF had many options for young recruits like him including a career path in electronics, and he wanted to choose that option.

His meeting with the recruitment officer went smoothly and the officer was more than helpful, arranging for his tests and physical. He even helped him find a motel nearby to stay until his recruitment papers were ready. Within a week, John had passed all the tests and had signed himself for a short term commission with the US Air Force and was on his way to a base near San Francisco for his basic training. After two years of training in the base, he was going to be commissioned in West Germany for the remaining four years of his commission. As he flew out of the DFW airport he realized that he had never made it into Dallas proper and that his life had taken an unexpected detour.

CHAPTER 3
John and Nicole

John's career in the Air Force had gone smoothly. He had passed all of his tests with flying colors and was liked by both his superiors and the other recruits. After two years of training at the California base, he was sent to a NATO base that was in a German town called Gilenkerchen. The base was dedicated to NATO Airborne Early Warning and Control and provided some state of the art opportunities for young recruits in electronics instrumentation. Knowing John's acute interest in electronic instrumentation, his supervisor at the California base had helped him get posted at Gilenkerchen. The base was in Teveren, a small town just outside of Gilenkerchen.

The new country, a new career, and new friends helped John evolve into a whole different person, and he had a much more enlightened view of life now. He could never take anything for granted from now on. He knew too well about the transitory nature of life and the tragic episode in Lubbock had only reinforced the temporal nature of life. He, however, was doing his best to forget that dreadful day. Moreover, he was trying hard to find his own purpose in life. While he knew that he was too young to find the answers right away, he was confident that some day, not too far into the future, he was bound to discover the answers.

The fact that he was far away from Texas helped him slowly erase his personal tragedy and heal his emotional scars. He knew he could never completely erase memories of that tragedy, but at least he was able to hide it deep inside his psyche. While that did stabilize his emotional status a lot, he still had occasional nightmares. One night, he was woken up by one of those recurring nightmares and could not go back to sleep. He just sat in his bed, motionless, wondering how he could stop getting those nightmares. As the dawn approached, he got up and took a long shower, hoping to forget that unpleasant nightmare.

While he was having his breakfast that morning, Gary, another young pilot, noticed that John's eyes were very red from lack of sleep. He had seen John like that several times in the past few months, but had never bothered to ask him about his sleeping problem lest he should be seen as too intrusive. This time, however, he could not keep quiet.

"What's the problem John? It looks like you didn't sleep last night. Your eyes are so red. Did you have some nightmare?"

"I'm OK, Gary. I have this problem once in a while when I can't fall asleep. No big deal." John replied trying hard to not make an issue out of his sleep disorder.

"That's all right, John. I just wanted to help you out. There are a few meditation techniques that can help you kick that problem you know," replied Gary.

That was the beginning of a budding friendship between the two. Gary Bartlett was from the New England area who had studied Eastern religions. He had practiced Yoga and meditation for a along time and was more than eager to teach John about meditation and how it could help him cope with his sleeping problems. Over the next few days, he not only taught some basic techniques of yoga and meditation, but he also gave him few books on the teachings of Buddha.

The more John read about Buddha, the more he was awestruck by the wisdom of Buddha's teachings. No wonder the ancient civilizations referred to Buddha as the Enlightened One, he mused. His teachings of the *Four Noble Truths* seemed so simple yet so powerful, and as he read them, he felt as if the Teacher himself were sitting next to him and explaining to him the deeper meanings ingrained in those truths. *Suffering exists* was the first noble truth and John knew very well about that truth. Is there any harsher suffering than losing one's parents at a young age? At that point, his misery seemed like the cruelest of all forms of sufferings. *Desire is the cause for suffering* was the next noble truth. The desire for love, protection, and the longing for recognition, they all were behind what Buddha had called collectively craving or desire. Buddha had proclaimed that *cessation from carving will lead one away from suffering* as the third noble truth. Finally, Buddha had revealed that *The Eight Fold Path* as the final noble truth that would lead one to *Nirvana*, or a state devoid of suffering. John felt terribly moved by Buddha's teachings, so much that he almost froze once he grasped the meaning of the Four Noble Truths. He was now convinced that it was the wisdom that Buddha had imparted on humanity specifically for troubled souls like him. He felt like a large tidal wave of wisdom had drenched him, and from that on, he was a committed follower of the Enlightened One. Years went by, and John found himself learning a lot not only about electronics but about life in general. He had read several books on Buddha and Zen, and meditation and yoga were now integral part of his morning routines. Gone were the nightmares and self-doubts about the purpose of life. While he wanted to be best in what he did, it was not because he was after some prize; and his motivation was driven by the Eight Fold Path, the right effort and the right focus. With his mind focused on the efforts, desire had become a non-existent element, and finding desire in John's heart was like finding an iceberg in a tropical sea.

When his commission was over, John was ready to go back to Texas. However, his plans to start a business related to the oil industry had to be reevaluated. It was 1986 and the oil prices had collapsed and several small companies related to the industry were closing shop. He realized that he had to pursue that dream sometime in the future as the timing was certainly important. However, his timing when it came to investments was perfect, and the money he had invested five years ago had grown to more than four hundred thousand dollars, providing him a comfortable financial cushion until he found a job. He wanted to go back to Dallas and look for a job in the defense industry knowing that his skills in electronics would be in high demand with defense contractors. Not surprisingly, the outplacement agency that helped USAF personnel returning to civilian life had lined up several interviews with defense contractors in the Dallas area, and John was confident that he would have a meaningful career once he went back to Texas. Gary was also coming close to the end of his commission and his plan was to join a commercial airliner as a pilot. John had encouraged him to join one of the airlines based in Dallas so that they could be near each other.

John decided to travel around Europe for a few weeks before going back to Dallas. He had, in fact, travelled around the continent every year during his vacation time as he had no close family back home. He had visited many major European cities including Rome, London, Athens, Paris and Monaco; his favorite, however, was Paris. He knew an old woman who rented rooms to American tourists at very reasonable rates, and that was where he stayed every time he went to Paris.

It was a hot, humid day, just like any other in the past week in Paris. After having a light lunch, John decided to visit the Versailles palace as he wanted to learn about revolutionary history. He took the train to the station that was a mile or so from the palace and walked the rest of the way. For the next four hours, he wandered around the palace admiring the rooms, the paintings, the furniture, and the history that went along with each piece. As he moved from room to room, the palace paintings were a reminder of the temporal nature of the material world; for him, the Versailles palace was like a museum that showcased Māya[7].

When John finally got out of the palace, he realized that he was very hungry. He looked at his watch; it was 7:00 in the evening. However, he knew that it was too early for most of the restaurants to be serving dinner. He remembered a Tex-Mex restaurant he had seen that was close to the station. So he decided to walk there, and see if they were serving dinner.

He got out of the huge parking lot next to the palace and started walking along the sidewalk of the large boulevard that was in front of the palace. He had walked for about ten minutes, when he saw a sign for "crepes", and as the place was already open, he decided to eat there.

As he entered the restaurant, he noticed that there were already many customers inside with a waitress who was busy

---

7   *Māya is the Divine energy or force that drives the material world.*

helping them. A middle aged man who looked like the chef himself came to help John and took him to a corner table that could seat two people. He also gave him a glass of some warm drink that tasted like apple cider and a menu that was in French.

John struggled to place an order as his knowledge of French was minimal to say the least. He wanted to order a couple of vegetarian crepes, and the man did not know much English either. Seeing their predicament, the young waitress came to John's table and offered to help him.

"I am Nicole, and I will help you with your order," Nicole introduced herself with a smile.

John noticed that she did not have a French accent, and soon realized that she was probably in Paris for a summer job.

"Thanks. I am John. I wanted to get some vegetarian crepes," John replied.

"Oh, you are a vegetarian? I am a vegetarian too," she replied.

"Well, not a strict vegetarian. I try to be whenever I can," replied John.

During that meal, John had found out that Nicole was from Holland, and was staying in Paris with a couple of friends for the summer. He also found out that she practiced Buddhism. She was slender with blue eyes and brown hair, and John felt attracted to her beyond his wildest imagination. He felt ridiculous to have developed such strong feelings for her just after few minutes, nay seconds, of conversation with her. He looked back at her and noticed that she was glancing at him which made him wonder if she had developed similar feelings towards him. As he ate his crepes, he wondered what had brought him to that particular restaurant at that specific time. Was it some sort of karma or destiny, he wondered.

After he had had finished his dinner and was ready to pay, he decided to ask her out.

"Nicole, can I ask you for a favor? I'm going to be in Paris for few days and I was wondering if you could come with me to see the city?" John asked Nicole.

"You mean, quit my job and be your guide?" she quipped with a smile.

"No, no. We could go out when you are not working," John was a little defensive.

"All right, that is a fair deal. I am not working tomorrow evening, and I live nearby. We can meet here tomorrow at 7 pm," Nicole replied, this time with a warm smile.

As they got to know each other, John found out that there were many similarities between them. Nicole had lost her parents in an accident when she was very little. She was raised by her aunt, her only relative. The loneliness had driven her to reading books, and one day when she was around twelve, she had come across a book about the teachings of Buddha. She was so moved by the teaching of The Enlightened One, she had cried through the night after she had finished the book. They were tears of joy as she had at last found a spiritual path that made her feel secure. Indeed, the teachings had made her feel serene. From that day, she had accepted the path laid down by The Enlightened One and had become a committed vegetarian. That was not her only passion; she had one more passion, which was tennis. She had played tennis at a competitive level and had represented her high school team.

After spending one week together, Nicole and John knew that they were deeply in love. In fact, John was convinced that he wanted to spend the rest of his life with her. As the time for is departure to Texas came near, he decided to ask her to marry him. Her reply, however, baffled him a little.

"I would very much like to marry you, John. However, there are things you do not know about me. If you knew, you might not want to marry me," replied Nicole.

"Are you talking about something about your past, Nicole? Nothing is going to change my mind," John was adamant about his decision.

"Well, I have a sickness. You may not want to live with someone who has that problem," Nicole replied, so softly that John thought that she was whispering.

"What type of sickness?"

"It is not a physical sickness," Nicole answered.

John did not say anything. He wondered what she was referring to as she looked perfectly fine to him.

"It comes on and off. I've been all right for the past two years thanks to my meditation," Nicole tried to explain.

"Whatever it is, I am willing to deal with it, Nicole. Please marry me," John pleaded.

John and Nicole were married twice; once in Holland with a small gathering of Nicole's friends and her Aunt and a second time in front of justice of peace in Dallas, Texas.

CHAPTER 4
The Early Years

John and Nicole were married and settled in Plano, a suburb at the northern edges of the Dallas Metroplex. John was now working for a defense contractor in Garland, another suburb of Dallas. He did not really enjoy his job; he found it to be rather boring as his real interest was to start a company that did seismic analysis for oil exploration. He knew very well that the oil business was a tough business for small producers, and his desire was to help small producers with affordable seismic analysis. He wanted to his company to help these producers maximize their oil output from their aging wells. However, 1986 was not a good year to start a company in the oil services business. Oil prices had collapsed, and Texas real estate, leveraged on the belief that oil prices would never come down, had collapsed along with the price of oil. Banks were closing and there was a sense of desperation all over Texas. Dallas had fared better than Houston and West Texas as its economy was much more diversified. John decided to wait for an opportune time to start his venture and to bide his time working for the defense contractor.

Although his work was not that exciting, John did not mind his job as it paid him well. Moreover, he had done fairly well with his investments which allowed him and Nicole to lead a comfortable life. Mr. Thompson, his adviser from Lubbock, had been right about the stock market. The interest rates had come down since their peak levels in 1981, and John's investments in stocks and bonds had soared. His investments along with his savings from the USAF days had made him an affluent man; not rich in the sense of oil and real estate tycoons that lived in Preston Hallow and Highland Park but more like a well to do middle class man. All of that did not matter to either John or Nicole as their needs were minimal, and their focus had nothing to do with money. They had bought a modest house in the southern edge of Plano and were now comfortably settled there.

While John worked in Garland, Nicole kept herself busy with a myriad of activities. She had joined a meditation group and had also started a Buddhist study group. To keep physically active, she was enrolled in the women's league at the Tennis Center in Plano, and she had started giving yoga classes in the evening at a local yoga center. While everything seemed normal, there was always the hidden fear in her mind that her mental state could shift and cause irreparable damage to her marital bliss. As much as she knew that John was a patient and understanding soul, beyond anyone's imagination, she was still not sure how he would handle it if the relapse did happen. But all those fears were just that – mere fears.

As Nicole sat in the dining room with her two kids and John, she thought how everything had turned out to be beautiful. She felt immeasurably thankful that none of her fears had come true, and she felt immensely proud how her two sons were growing up to be wonderful boys.

Her first son was, John II, was seven years old and was a perfect child in every way. Her second son Johan was now five years who was a little moody and exhibited introvert tendencies. At times, Nicole found him to be difficult to understand. John II was affectionately called Junior and his favorite sport was football. He wanted to play football for A&M, his father's Alma matter, when he went to college. While Junior was a perfect student who got the best grades and always did everything right to please his parents, Johan was at times rebellious and would get into uncontrollable tantrums. If Nicole tried to discipline him, he would dive into an introvert state when he would not talk to anyone for hours and sometimes for days. Nicole worried that something was terribly wrong with Johan's mind; she even wondered if he had developed some sort of psychological syndrome. At times she wondered if she was to blame for that since she always compared Johan's abilities in school and sports to that of Junior's which no doubt irritated Johan. The comparison would always end with Nicole making the same statement.

"Why can't you be more like Junior, Johan?"

Of course, little Johan resented that, and would give his mom a puzzled look whenever she said that. His never understood why his mother said things like that.

One day when Johan was alone with his dad, he garnered enough courage to ask his dad about this.

"Dad, why does Mom always say that I'm not as good as Junior? What does she mean by that?"

That question troubled John beyond limits, and his eyes became somewhat moist. He looked away from Johan for few seconds to get his thoughts together. He then took hold of little Johan and made him sit on his lap.

"Johan, you need to realize that mom sometimes says things that she really does not mean. You just have to trust me on that. There is no one in this world she loves more than you," assured John softly as he ran his fingers through Johan's hair.

That simple assurance gave Johan tremendous confidence, and he knew he could always trust his dad as John had never said anything that had made him feel bad. Instinctively, Johan hugged his dad, and they stayed like that for a long time.

CHAPTER 5
Johan's Visions

Years went by quickly, and Johan was now ten years old. His interest in tennis as a sport had increased every year so much so that he often dreamed of being a professional player. It was a dream that often intensified whenever he was watching a grand slam tournament on television like the one he was watching right now. However, he was not very confident about this prospect as he was too frail and lacked the ability to focus. There was a secret that he had been jealously guarding that had kept him from focusing on anything, let alone tennis. He shivered when he thought about this. He turned his attention to the match on the TV to distract from that thought.

When that did not help, Johan looked out of the window. It was a pleasant autumn afternoon in Plano, Texas; the sky was clear blue and temperature outside was a pleasant seventy five degree. Finally, his endless staring at the sky calmed him down.

Nicole and Johan were watching one of the earlier rounds of US Open. Federer had just won his third round match and from the way he was playing there was no doubt that he was on his way to win yet another US Open title. While they were watching the match, John had gone to his office as he had to attend to some important business. He had to meet with one of his clients and deliver his report on the feasibility of opening an old oil well. There were too many projects like that one on his hand as the booming oil price had enticed many investors to look into the possibility of reopening old oil wells. Knowing that the oil business was subject to unpredictable economic vagaries, Nicole did not mind her husband working overtime during the weekends.

Nicole did not find anything interesting in the next match that had just come on the television. She looked outside through the window and decided that it was a good time to take Johan and coach him on his ground strokes.

"Johan, do you want to go out to the tennis center and hit some balls?" she asked Johan.

Johan did not mind that, in fact he was more than eager to play tennis, but the only thing that made him hesitate was the way she could react to his performance.

Nicole had always wanted Johan to be a successful tennis player. She herself had started coaching him in tennis when he had turned just four. She had him play local tournaments when he was as young as seven year old. Unfortunately, to her disappointment, Johan never excelled in tennis, and in spite of years of coaching by his mother, he never graduated from the lowest level of the USTA tennis level for juniors.

Johan was a frail kid who was severely challenged when it came to long term focus. While he was quick and knew all the technical skills of a good player, he always ended up losing matches, sometimes to players who were not even close to him in technical abilities. As tennis was a sport that demanded intense focus, he would invariably make errors as it was impossible for him to focus on the ball for more than a minute. He was always distracted by strange visions during his matches especially when he tried to focus on the ball.

He never told his parents about his visions as he was afraid that they would think that there was something wrong with him. He had once watched a movie on the TV where a boy was in a similar situation, and when the boy had told his parents about his strange visions in his head, his parents had concluded that the boy was possessed by spirits which had led to untold complications for the family. Johan did not want anything like that to happen to him, and his ultimate fear was that his parents would abandon him because of the unexplainable visions inside his head. The fear of abandonment had made him keep his secret to himself, and he had never told anyone about it, not even his parents.

"I will go with you, Mom. But please don't get upset if my focus drops off," replied Johan.

"No, Johan, I won't be upset as long as you do your best," Nicole replied as she grabbed her car keys that were on the end table.

"Do we have courts reserved?" Johan asked. As soon as he asked that, he knew that it was an unnecessary question. His mom always reserved courts on Sunday afternoons.

Nicole rented a cart of tennis balls and started her lesson with Johan. He was hitting the ball quite well and was consistently making his shots. This only increased her frustration as she was unable to explain why her son was not able to win important matches. She knew it had to do more with mental toughness as tennis was a sport that required both physical talent and mental toughness.

The first 30 minutes of the lesson went so well that Nicole was greatly pleased. She hoped that her son would be able to win the next month tournament and qualify for the next level.

"Let us take a small break and work on your backhand next, Johan. Why don't you get all the balls back into the cart," suggested Nicole.

When Nicole resumed the lesson, she was in a good mood seeing how well Johan had done during the first part of the lesson. *I hope he can maintain his concentration at today's level during the next tournament,* she kept telling herself.

"You are doing very well, Johan. If you can keep up this level of focus, you should be a superchamp in no time," she tried to encourage Johan.

Then all of a sudden it happened again; the visions – the visions of blazing flames – started messing up his focus. These were the same visions that had sporadically surfaced in his head for the last few years. First he thought that they were just nightmares that would go away, and when they kept reappearing, he knew that there was a strange, perhaps, a deeper reason behind those visions. He, however, was afraid to ask anyone about them, not even his mom and dad.

He could see a large complex of medieval buildings bursting into flames with hundreds of ancient structures crumbling. There was unbelievable mayhem everywhere and he could see orange clad monks running for their lives. There was a powerful army chasing the monks who kept falling to the ground as the soldiers butchered them, and some were being beheaded mercilessly. He saw an old monk coming out of a large building that looked like the most important building in the complex. The monk was saying something to a general who looked very angry as he drew his sword and severed the monk's head. It was all too much for young Johan, and he kept trembling inside as he could even feel the heat emanating from the blazing flames. He tried to hide his feelings and tried to hit the ball that his mother had hit into his court, but he was off balance and made an error.

Nicole did not pay much attention to it as that was the first error he had made during that session. However, it was no different with the next few shots and errors kept piling up. Johan could not focus any more as he was confused and kept perspiring. On one hand, he did not know why those visions kept recurring and he had no idea what they meant or if they had any significance, and on the other hand, he was afraid that his mother was going to have an outburst at his demonstration of lack of focus.

A frustrated Nicole slowly walked towards his side of the court where Johan sheepishly waited for her.

"What is the matter, Johan? Why can't you play like you were playing earlier? What happened to your focus?" Nicole tried to be calm and was trying her best to control her anger.

Johan looked down and kept staring at his tennis sneakers and avoided any eye contact with his mother. He nervously flung his racket and refused to say anything which only infuriated Nicole further. Was it the right time to confide about his secret? Johan wondered secretly. Deep inside, he knew that he had to tell his mom about his visions some time or the other; he could not hide it anymore, and he only hoped that she would understand. He prayed that she would not think that there was something wrong with his mind.

"I do not know, Mom. I keep getting these visions that make me lose my focus," he tried to explain very slowly, so slowly that he almost swallowed the word visions.

"What type of visions?" Nicole sounded confused.

"There are these buildings on fire. There are monks murdered with blood all over. I see soldiers who are killing thousands of people. I am scared, Mom," Johan tried to explain.

Nicole was perplexed, and her immediate reaction was that Johan was making up some fancy story as an excuse for his sloppy performance. She worried that one of his favorite wacky cartoon shows had finally corroded his thinking.

Seeing that his mom was not convinced, Johan got even more worried.

"It's true, Mom, and I'm not making it up. Please don't think that I'm crazy," Johan pleaded.

Nicole concluded that it was all an act. "Okay, Johan. If you don't want to continue with your lesson any more, just tell me that. You do not have to make up these wild excuses," she replied sternly and walked towards the center of the court and started picking up her bag.

"Go and get all the balls. We're going home," she turned back and yelled at Johan.

Johan was extremely unhappy with what had transpired in those few minutes. He looked at the sky and noticed that the visions were all gone, and all he could see was the wide, blue Texas sky.

As he brought back the tennis balls to the cart, Nicole was still seething.

"You know Johan, with the type of attitude you have, you are never going to be any good in tennis," she scolded him as she slammed her bag into the cart.

She had raised her voice considerably and people in nearby courts could hear her now. Johan was now really worried that his mother would make an embarrassing scene.

Fortunately, for him, she quickly returned the cart and they were both inside the car as she started speeding the car towards home. Neither of them said anything to each other, and Johan was perfectly happy with that eerie silence.

They were going south on the US 75 access road toward their home, when she finally broke out of her silence.

"I will drop you at home and go and see your brother practice football. At least he isn't a disappointment."

Johan did not say anything. He knew that every time she mentioned his brother, it was bad news, and the less he said anything, the better it was.

As soon as they reached home, she stopped the car in front of the house, let Johan into the house, and locked the house behind him.

Within minutes, she was speeding her car again towards the Clark Stadium where high schools football practices were held.

Johan went to his room and fell on his bed and closed his eyes as he was scared and worried and did not know what to do. He held his pillow tight as if it was his last support and he hoped that his dad would come back home soon so that he did not have to feel so lonely. The more he thought about his situation, the more he got scared. He was scared about his recurring visions, but more than that, he was scared that something was utterly wrong with his mother.

As he lay on the bed wondering what to do next, he sensed that a dark shadow had blanketed his room. Alarmed, he looked outside and noticed the clouds gathering above signaling an impending storm. Out of curiosity, he sat on the bed and stared at the window to see what was going on. As he looked outside through the window he had a surreal experience and could sense that everything around him was melting which rendered him motionless. First it was the window and then the ceiling and finally the walls - they were all gone and suddenly, he was standing alone in an open field, and the sky was clear again. He knew immediately that he was having a vision, albeit a different one this time. This time, there were no sounds of a marching army, there was no towering inferno, nor were there any killings or blood streams. This time it was calm and he could sense that he was at the bottom of a mountain range. He looked up and saw the distant snow covered peaks, and he could even hear the sounds of nature including the soothing sound of the flowing water streams nearby. Then it happened in a flash. The whole area was covered with a dense fog, and out of the fog came a man who looked both old and young at the same time. He was skinny with no fat whatsoever on his body. He had long flowing silvery hair that touched his shoulders, and his beard was long and silvery. He looked like a yogi he had read about in a story book. Johan wondered why this yogi was in his vision. Johan figured that the man was very old, perhaps more than one hundred years. Yet, when he looked at his face, there was not even a single wrinkle; his skin was shiny and smooth.

The man came to him and addressed Johan directly.

"Johan, I see that you are very scared," said the yogi.

Johan nodded his head in agreement with the yogi.

"You are scared about the vision you are having?"

Johan nodded his head again. Right now, however, he was worried about his mother.

"You are more worried about your mother right now, right?" the yogi added as if he had read Johan's mind.

"I am very worried about my mom. Is she going to be all right?" Johan garnered enough courage to ask the yogi. The yogi did not answer, making Johan even more worried.

"Your mother wants you to be a tennis star. I can help you with that," the yogi added.

Johan's eyes opened wide when he heard that.

"You can help me with my tennis?" Johan replied in disbelief. "Who are you, why are you trying to help me?" added Johan as he got more comfortable with the vision.

"I am a yogi you will meet sometime in the future. When we do, I will explain all about those strange visions you are having," explained the yogi. "For the time being, we will focus on your tennis. Your mother will no longer be displeased with your tennis," assured the yogi.

Johan felt relieved. He still wanted one more clarification which was really a cry for more of an assurance. "Will those scary visions stop coming?" he asked the yogi, hoping for an affirmative answer.

"They will, Johan. They will not bother you anymore." The yogi assured Johan as he slowly disappeared into the fog.

Just then, Johan heard a creaking noise as his dad John opened the door to his room. The noise jolted Johan, and just like it had happened so many times before, his vision was gone in a flash, and he was back in his room sitting on his bed. Johan was extremely pleased to see his dad.

"Johan, why are you alone here? Where is mom?" John sounded concerned as Johan rushed to hug his dad.

He hugged his dad and stood still not saying even a single word. Finally, when he was sure that he was really back in the present time, Johan replied.

"Mom went to the football field. She said she wanted to watch the football practice." Johan did not want to mention his brother.

"Did she say anything else?" John enquired. "What else did she say?" John repeated the question as Johan looked down not willing to say anything.

"Let us go and get your mother," John took Johan's hand and they both rushed to John's car.

In less than ten minutes, they were near the stadium. John asked Johan to stay in the car and started walking towards the stadium which was empty except for Nicole who was sitting right at the center of the middle section. Nicole smiled when she saw John and started coming down the stadium. She then ran to John and hugged him with tears flowing over her cheeks. They stayed there for several minutes as Johan sat in the car hoping everything was all right with his mother.

When they came back to the car, Nicole seemed to be in good spirit. "We had a very good practice today. I had never seen Johan hit the ball so well before," she said, giving her assessment to John.

Johan thought that it was the right time to show his new found confidence to his mom.

"Mom, you are never going to be unhappy with my tennis again. I will be a super champ soon," Johan declared.

Nicole ran her fingers through Johan's hair and declared softly, "I know, I know. Something tells me that everything is going to be all right."

CHAPTER 6
Yogi the Coach

Johan's tennis prowess started to blossom from the very next time he stepped on the court. Perhaps, because of the assurance given by the yogi, he was no longer worried about the scary vision that was distracting his focus. His renewed confidence along with his new found focus improved his game tremendously so much that he started winning all of his matches easily. Within six months, he graduated to the USTA champ level, and within a year he was playing in the superchamp level for boys who were twelve years of age and under. Month by month, his ranking kept improving and he was finally ranked among the top 50 players in Texas. Indeed, he never looked back, and when he graduated to the next age group, he retained his superchamp level. Both of his parents were pleased with his progress, and Nicole was so delighted with his success that she stopped making comparisons to Junior.

Something else had changed in his life as well; it was now more than two years since the yogi had communicated with him. The recurring visions of inferno were gone and Johan's life was as normal as it could be, and yet, deep inside Johan was troubled that the yogi had made no attempt to contact him again. Did he not promise that he was going to be Johan's coach? He had indeed promised him that he was going to teach him about secrets of tennis; secrets that would make him play like no other tennis player. Or was this just an inspirational speech to get Johan to find his innate talent and develop on his own? Every time he thought about the yogi, he felt disappointed and sad. It was as though there was now a big void in his life. What amazed him most was that such a brief interaction with the yogi had made such a large impression on him, and he kept longing for the yogi to appear in his dreams again.

Johan was now fourteen year old and was a freshman in high school. He was getting taller and gaining strength at a rapid pace; and he no longer looked like a weak kid although he was still lanky. His dedication and focus had improved every aspect of his tennis game; his speed and footwork were amazing and his serve and volley techniques had shown remarkable progress. He still had problems with his baseline game, especially when bigger kids overpowered him with deep ground strokes. In tense rallies, the point often ended with him committing an error which frustrated him endlessly. He knew very well that without a solid baseline game, he was not going to reach the top ten in Texas among the boys in his age group. He tried to compensate for his weakness at baseline by serve and volleying, and while that strategy worked against most of the players, it was suicidal against players who had excellent ground strokes combined with speed. The result was always the same whenever he played against top tier players in his group: him losing badly as the match progressed. The score never looked that bad; his opponent would only win one or two of Johan's services games. It was the emotional let down that made each loss seem unbearable, and he felt like he had hit a wall and needed more help. He was no longer sure that his mom's coaching was sufficient for him to rise to the next level.

Johan and Nicole were on their way to Waco to play the December superchamp tournament. It was always his mom who took him to out of town matches as John was always busy with his work even during the weekends. Johan hoped to do well enough to be selected for the next month's superchamp excellence tournament. Only the top twenty eight players were eligible to play in the tournament.

"You know, Johan, if you reach even the semi-finals you will have enough points to qualify for the superchamp excellence." Nicole made a casual observation as she kept her focus on the traffic.

Johan took his headphones out and turned off his music, realizing that his mom was telling him something.

"Did you say something, Mom?"

"Yes, I was just calculating the points you would accumulate if you went to the semis," she replied.

Johan had stopped paying too much attention to his points as it often made him nervous during important matches.

"Will that be enough for me to qualify for the excellence tournament, Mom?"

"Yes, it will. Remember, you meet number three seed in the quarter finals, and if you beat him, you will get quite a few points," Nicole explained.

She hoped that this would give him an extra motivation to play hard against the number three seed.

Johan played very well in that tournament and easily won the first three rounds. As anticipated, his next round was the quarter final match against the number three seed. Johan played his best during the match and won the first set. However, his opponent recovered and pinned Johan down at the baseline for the next two sets never giving him a chance to come to the net. With his superior ground strokes, he beat Johan with a comfortable margin in the next two sets.

After the match, he slowly walked towards his mom, placed his tennis bag next to her, and stood there without saying a word. Johan felt helpless, and a sense of failure engulfed him. He felt miserable knowing that he had utterly disappointed his mother. Even more hurtful was that he had hit a seemingly invisible wall that prevented him from progressing any further with his tennis dreams. He was so ashamed that he avoided eye contact with Nicole.

"You played amazingly well, Johan. We will work on your ground strokes, and next time you play him, you will be able to beat him." Nicole tried to encourage him.

Johan did not say anything and just stared at the matches that were in progress at other courts. He knew that there was no point in staying in Waco that night, and it was time for them to check out of the hotel.

"Mom, can I stay here and watch Nick's match while you check out from the hotel?" Johan pleaded to his mother.

Nicole understood that her son wanted to be left alone and walked towards her car as Johan went towards the court where Nick was playing his quarter final match.

Nick was a consistent player who never made mental mistakes, and his game was neither flashy nor overpowering. However, he was an intelligent player who had enough tactics to force his opponents make unforced errors. This strategy made him consistently win matches until he faced a superior player. This match was no different as Nick easily won it with a smart strategy.

Johan walked with Nick towards the official where Nick reported the score and later they both walked to the club house. Nick knew that Johan had lost his match just by looking at his eyes. They both needed some rest as they sat in a corner to avoid the crowd.

"What happened? Was it your baseline game that failed you again?"

"I don't seem to get the range when hitting from the base line," Johan sighed.

"Have you tried practicing with the machine?"

"I've tried everything. Nothing seems to help me. Only the yogi can help," Johan slipped and inadvertently mentioned the yogi.

"What do you mean by 'the yogi'?" Nick smiled and looked half puzzled and half curious.

Johan did not know what to say. He had to think about something quick to defuse Nick's curiosity.

"Oh, I read about this yogic power that will let you accomplish anything, walk on water or even fly," Johan replied with a smile.

"Oh, that type of yogic power. Let me know when you get that, and I've always wanted to be able to fly," Nick replied laughing.

They were chatting for almost thirty minutes when Nicole came to the area where they were sitting.

"Hi, Nick, how did you do in your match?" she asked Nick as she approached them.

"I won. I hope to do well in the semis. I have never won a semi-final, you know," he replied.

"You will, Nick," Nicole assured him and then turned to Johan. "Johan if we start now, we should be in Dallas before dark."

Nicole was anxious to get back home before it got too dark. They bid goodbye to Nick and got into the car and were soon driving north on I-35 towards Dallas. Johan was exhausted from the match and decided to stretch his feet and take a nap. As he slowly dozed off, his only wish was that he could connect with the yogi again.

That night, Johan went to bed early and was deep asleep in his room when he felt a slight breeze over his face. It felt warm like a mid-summer breeze which was strange given that it was December. What was even stranger was that he remembered that he had closed the window before he went to bed. He got up and tried to look at the window to see if it had opened. To his astonishment, he was no longer in his room. He was in a tropical place with an unspoiled meadow, and he saw a trail that led to the end of the meadow towards a group of trees. He instinctively started following the trail.

Johan knew that he was dreaming but desperately hoped that his dream would take him to the yogi. He did not want to wake up before he had met the yogi and discussed his game with him.

As he came close to the group of trees, he noticed that the yogi was standing beneath one of the trees as if he was waiting for Johan.

"I am glad you came here, Johan," the yogi welcomed him with a smile.

"I am the one who is happy and excited, Yogi. I never thought that I would see you again," Johan replied, trying to control his excitement. He was tempted to ask the yogi why he had not come to him for such a long time but was afraid to do so.

"I know, you are wondering why I did not visit you earlier. Let me just say that I wanted to see you develop your tennis on your own before it was time for me to help you," the yogi answered.

He then took Johan towards a medium-sized boulder and asked him to climb it. The boulder was hardly four feet tall and Johan had no problem in quickly climbing the boulder.

"I want you to sit down in the lotus position and start meditating. I want you to breath rhythmically as you meditate," the yogi instructed Johan.

As Johan sat in the lotus position and started meditating, he could hardly focus. While he went through the rhythmic breathing without any problem, his mind was cluttered with too many thoughts. Thoughts connected with mom, dad, school, Nick, homework, and so on crept randomly into his mind. The yogi could see the lines of tension on Johan's face.

The yogi put his left palm on Johan's head and moved his right palm over his face as if to cleanse his mind of all unnecessary thoughts.

"I want to you to meditate on this mantra, Johan. As you exhale, I want you to repeat this mantra in silence – *Om Namo Nārāyana*," the yogi instructed, still with his left palm over Johan's head.

Johan continued his meditation repeating the mantra as he exhaled. To his amazement, his mind was now devoid of any thoughts whatsoever, and he slowly felt liberated and free as he had never felt before. It was like each time he exhaled with the mantra, his mind was being cleansed, which brought him amazing clarity, and soon, he felt like he was floating in air. He did not know how long he was in that position, but when he finally heard the yogi's voice, it was as if it came from deep inside his own mind.

"It is now time for you to focus on the tennis ball as you meditate," yogi's voice instructed Johan.

A spinning yellow tennis ball appeared in front of Johan, and the ball was spinning so fast that Johan had a hard time focusing on the ball.

"I want you to completely focus on the ball. The more you focus the more you can see, and your concentration will appear to slow the spinning of the ball," the yogi explained.

Johan struggled as he tried to completely concentrate on the ball. It was only after several attempts at it, he was finally able to concentrate fully on the ball. As his focus increased, the ball's spinning slowed. In the end it had almost stopped spinning.

At that point, the yogi put his palm on John's head and asked him to come out of his meditation.

"You are done for the day. We will continue with this for a few more sessions, and when you master your concentration, I will take you to the court," the yogi explained and then as he slowly disappeared into thin air as he bid good bye to Johan.

Johan slowly opened his eyes and stared at the ceiling, wondering if he had really travelled thousands of miles to meet the yogi. *Was it my soul that had just made this incredible journey*, he wondered. Nevertheless, he felt exhilarated like never before, and he felt like the last piece of the puzzle was falling into the right place. He was so excited that he wanted to share his secret with someone, someone he could trust. However, he was afraid to tell his mom or dad lest they should conclude that something was wrong with him. He really did not want to make his parents worry about him, and the only one he could trust was his friend Nick. When he met Nick the next time during a practice session, he confided in Nick about his dream. Nick's immediate reaction was to brush it off as one of those wild dreams, but he promised to keep it a secret.

Johan had the same dream three more times and with each dream his level of concentration improved. When the yogi was finally satisfied with his progress, he was ready to teach Johan the next set of lessons. The fourth time they met, the yogi took him into an area which was completely covered by a dense fog. As they entered the fog and moved deeper into the area, it became apparent to Johan that they were on a tennis court, and Johan saw a mysterious player at far end of the court. He tried to see if he could recognize the other player, but to his frustration, the face appeared blurred.

"Don't worry about him. He is going to play a set with you, and during that set I want you to focus on the ball with the same intensity as during your meditation. Other than that, just play your game," the yogi advised as he handed him a racquet.

Johan gingerly entered the court and waited for the stranger at the other end to start rallying. He decided to do what the yogi and told him; he was completely focused on the ball. To his amazement, he noticed that although the other player was hitting very hard, the ball did not seem to be traveling very fast. Even more amazing was that he could see the rotation of the ball as it came towards him, and he could even see his racket striking the ball as he practiced his strokes.

After a few minutes of warming up, they began their first game. Johan was in complete focus and did not miss a shot; he handled the deep powerful shots that were sent towards the corners of the court by his opponent with ease and confidence. They were both hitting the ball so well that each point went on for several minutes. In the end, they were tied at 40-40, but he soon lost the next point and it was advantage his opponent. He would lose the game if he did not win the next point, but he was determined to not let that happen. He focused on the ball and played as hard as he could. He could see the ball so well that all of his shots were perfectly timed and placed. After an exchange of several shots, Johan hit a deep powerful backhand cross court. He was confident that he had pinned his opponent in the corner, and the only way for his opponent to salvage was to resort to a short cross court shot which he planned to pounce on with his monstrous forehand shot. To his bewilderment, his opponent went around the ball in a flash and ripped a down-the-line shot that came back so fast that Johan hardly had any time to adjust his position. Before he could even get back to the center of the baseline, the ball zipped by like a bullet. Johan has lost the game and felt exhausted and was utterly disappointed. He dropped his racket and looked down at his feet in disbelief and stood there in that position for several seconds. Finally, when he looked up, his opponent was gone, and there was no one other than himself on the court.

"Don't worry, Johan. You are doing all right." The yogi tried to comfort him.

"Why did I lose then, Yogi?" Johan sounded puzzled.

"You need to raise your concentration level even further. When you do that you will see tunnels of light that will follow the ball. These tunnels will tell you where the ball will be coming back. That way, your opponent will find it almost impossible to hit winners against you," the yogi explained. "Now go back and play another game against him."

When Johan looked up again, he saw the stranger waiting for him at the other end of the court.

This time, Johan worked harder to concentrate on the ball, and just as the yogi had told him, he began to see tunnels of light as the ball traversed from one side to the other. First he saw only the tunnel from his side to the other side. However, after a while as he hit the ball, he not only saw the tunnel of light that went from his side to the opponent's side, he began to notice the second tunnel of light that came from his opponents side to his side of the court. This told him where he had to be to face the return shot which enabled him to be in a perfect position to hit winners. This time he easily won the game, and he felt a sense of gratification.

He looked towards the yogi to see if he could sense his feedback. The yogi looked at him and nodded in approval, something that thrilled Johan.

"That should be enough for the day, Johan. We will practice for the next several days, and when you play in your next tournament, you should have no problem winning the whole thing," the yogi assured.

For the next several nights, the dream continued with the yogi, helping Johan fine-tune his concentration skills to a level of perfection. Johan was now supremely confident about his abilities and could not wait for the next tournament.

CHAPTER 7
Air Turbulence

I felt a sudden jolt as our plane to Chicago started experiencing strong turbulence, waking me up. I could hear the pilot asking passengers to return to their seats and to make sure that their seat belts were fastened, and I could also hear him assuring the passengers that the turbulence was not going to last for a long time. I looked around and saw that the cabin was dimly lighted with most of the passengers asleep. I looked to my right and saw that Johan was deep asleep as well. Or was he?

I was still struggling to understand the story he had told me so far. He had mentioned his mother was missing but had not told me the details. What were the circumstances that led to her disappearance? He had barely mentioned details about his elder brother Junior, and there was Nick, his best friend; and very few details about Nick had been narrated to me. How was I going to put together the story if key pieces were missing? If Nick is his best friend, should he not tell me more about his background?

"There is no need to be stressed out, Mysore," I heard Johan's voice. "I will tell you all the details, and it will all be clear in due time. There will be plenty of material for you to write the book. I am afraid that you may not be able to finish the story in one book."

"You mean, I will have to write a sequel to complete your story?"

"Perhaps, you may even need to write a trilogy," explained Johan.

I felt reassured and wanted Johan to continue with the story. Right at that moment our plane shook abruptly, throwing me off balance, I grabbed Johan's hand spontaneously for support. It was at that moment that I experienced the strange vision that Johan had mentioned to me in his narrative. I was thrown into some medieval time. I heard the march of the cavalry. There were warriors wielding swords and lancers all around me. There was so much dust around me that I could barely see what was going on. I could hear some strange war cry in a foreign tongue that sounded like howling. I saw monks running for their lives as the warriors chased them and beheaded them with wild swings of their swords, causing streams of blood to flow. I sat down and covered my head with both hands, afraid that one of those swings would kill me. The fear for my life was intense, and I started perspiring profusely. Although I knew that the whole thing was an illusion, I felt scared and started praying. My prayers were soon answered and everything was restored back to normal. It all had happened in less than a minute, but I was soaking wet from my perspiration. I turned to Johan who was now awake and stared into his face.

"Is this the vision you had as a child?"

Johan nodded his head affirmatively. I felt a chill in down my spine as I tried to recollect the vision I had experienced only moments earlier. I could now understand first hand how terrifying it must have been for the young Johan. I wanted to know his story more than before and felt that I was now an integral part of this unfolding mystery.

"Could you please continue with your narrative?" I pleaded to Johan.

"I will, I will. Let me tell you that right now I myself do not know how this story ends."

CHAPTER 8
Disappearance

The dreams where Johan had personal coaching sessions by the yogi had an enormous impact on Johan's tennis skills. He was now more confident and more focused than ever before. He kept winning matches one after another and soon he was among the top ten boys in his age level. He had now graduated to the sixteen-and-under age group as he was now fifteen years old.

Both Nicole and John were extremely happy with his progress. Indeed, Nicole was the happiest and Johan's success made her less moody and melancholic, pleasing John infinitely.

Several companies were vying to sponsor Johan and were ready to take care of Johan's tennis needs, including his equipment, coaching, and travel expenses. John and Nicole had chosen a famous footwear company to be Johan's sponsor. That summer in the Texas Grand Slam held annually in College Station, Johan defeated all of his opponents in the sixteen and under age group including the number one and two seeds. He played so well in the finals that the spectators and scouts were supremely impressed. Indeed, everyone who watched the match that evening realized that they were witnessing the birth of a tennis star.

That evening, John, Nicole and Johan, who were staying at the College Station Hilton, decided to go to a nearby local Mexican restaurant to celebrate Johan's success. They got down from the elevator and started walking towards the door when a man walked up to them with a big smile.

"Congratulations, Johan. You played really well today," the man said, shaking Johan's hand. He then looked towards John and Nicole, and introduced himself. "Hi, I am Reggie Walker. I am a scout for your sponsor. I was talking with my manager and when I told him how well Johan plays, he came up with some fantastic ideas."

John and Nicole smiled and waited for him to continue.

"I would like to sit down and discuss the details with you. Can we do that tomorrow morning during breakfast?" Reggie requested.

"Sure, we can certainly do that," John replied.

"Can we meet here in the café at 8:30 am?"

"Sound good. It was nice meeting you, Reggie," John replied as they walked towards the parking lot.

All during the dinner Johan was curious what Reggie had in mind; what were those "fantastic ideas" his sponsor had? Nevertheless, he kept quiet as not to appear too eager. Nicole was excited too as she knew that the next couple of years would be breakthrough period for Johan. Johan could hardly sleep that night.

When they all got together the next morning for breakfast, Reggie slowly explained the ideas his company had. They would take Johan to a topnotch coach where he would coach Johan one on one. Johan would periodically practice with few elite players to hone his newly acquired skills. After one year of intense training, he would start playing in the junior circuit in Europe. One to two years in the junior circuit, and he would be ready to play as a fully pledged professional.

As Reggie explained his plans, John and Nicole listened intently without saying anything. Johan, however, wanted to know more.

"Who is this coach? Where is he?" he asked.

"He is a coach in Florida," Reggie replied smiling at Johan.

"But I already have a coach," Johan replied reflexively, not caring if he was being rude or not.

"This coach is very special. He has coached many world number ones," Reggie replied smilingly.

But I do not need any coach. No coach is better than my yogi, Johan mused. This time he was careful to hold his thoughts to himself, however.

"That means Johan will have to live alone in Florida?" Nicole sounded anxious.

"We will take care of all of his requirements. He will be with a few other elite kids. You can visit him any time you want, Nicole. We will cover all expenses," Reggie tried to allay her anxiety.

The discussion went on for few more minutes with Nicole and Johan quizzing Reggie for more details. As they finished breakfast, John summarized their collective response for all the three.

"Thanks for the information, Reggie. We will digest what you have told us and get back to you with our decision."

"I agree with you one hundred percent. This is not something you rush into. I will call back in a couple of weeks, if that is OK with you." Reggie was a no pressure salesman, and he understood that a decision such as this required some serious thinking.

John and Nicole had several weeks of discussions to decide about Johan's tennis career. They were both reluctant to send him off to a distant coach as they were not sure about his ability to handle emotional stress of being away from home. Further, John was in no position to accompany Johan and Nicole as his business had hit high gear due to soaring oil prices. He was also worried about Nicole's health. His conclusion was that for that next eighteen months, Johan was better off working with a local coach they had recently recruited to help their son.

Johan had just returned home from a long practice session, and he went straight up to his bath room for a long shower. That had become his new routine. Rigorous practice followed by a hot shower and an early dinner. When he came back to the kitchen for his dinner, he saw that both his parents were waiting for him at the kitchen table.

"Johan, come and sit down with us. We want to talk to you about Reggie's proposal," Joan waved his son towards the table.

"You mean the guy we met in College Station," Johan replied as he sat next to his parents.

"Yes, that is exactly what we want to discuss. After some careful evaluation, both your mother and I think that we should wait for a while before we commit to something serious like that," John tried to explain the decision ever so gently. Both Johan and Nicole were concerned that Johan might be disappointed with their decision.

"That is all right dad. I do not need any coach right now. You call and tell that to Reggie," Johan smiled, got up and walked back to the kitchen counter to check on the dinner.

Several months had passed since that conversation. Johan had progressed well in his career and was now playing at national level tournaments in places like California, Florida and New York. The progress was remarkable as he consistently beat top talents in the country. The obvious advice John and Nicole got from the coaches after Johan won those tournaments was to prepare him for an eventual professional career. *Why not send him to a top notch tennis academy in Florida or California?* was the usual comment. John and Nicole knew that they had to make a decision soon. Johan had just turned sixteen, and it was time for them to finally make the decision about the next move.

It was a late spring afternoon, and Nicole sat on a patio chair in the backyard enjoying the mild Texas sun. She was happy that Johan's tennis career had taken off just like the way she had dreamed. Unfortunately, Junior's path had taken an unexpected turn which was always troubling in her mind. After he had finished his high school, she had hoped that Junior would attend Texas A&M just like his dad. She had even hoped that he would be selected to play in their football team. During the summer after his high school graduation that dream had come to a crash. One day Junior came back from a visit to a friend's house to make a surprise announcement.

"Mom, I have a surprise for you," Junior had declared.

"What is it? I hope it is something good," Nicole sounded anxious as she did not like surprises.

"Congratulate me Mom. I have just signed up to join the Marines," Junior said with a beaming smile, and he seemed very proud of his decision.

Nicole froze as she heard those words. She refused to believe her own ears. "Did you say US marines?"

"Yes, Mom. I want to go to Iraq and help make this world a safer place."

Nicole cried for hours after failing to convince Junior to change his mind. She had begged John to convince Junior but that had not worked either. She was now resigned to him being in Iraq and hoped every day that he would be safe.

She tried to relax and put her mind at ease. She always enjoyed spring time afternoons in Dallas. Temperature was still mild and the sky was clear. Fortunately there was no sign of any spring storm that sometimes brought torrential rains to Dallas.

She stared at the pool and the multiple fountains in the spa. The sound of the fountains along with the waterfall at the edge of the pool made a rhythmic sound that soothed her. She closed her eyes, trying to meditate and sat in that position for a long time.

After a while she decided to go back and turn on the TV. It was some news channel that was showing scenes from the Iraq war which frightened her. There were two guests on the TV channel who were arguing about the morality of Iraq war. Periodically they were flashing scenes from Crawford, Texas where a group of people were protesting against the war. The protest was led by a woman who had lost her son in the war.

In her mind, there was nothing more terrible than war, and there was nothing moral about them. All wars are man-made and brought out the worst in human civilization. She had heard arguments about "just" wars. Perhaps the Second World War as one such just war; but was that preventable?

The guest was arguing that the Iraq war was a just war. It was not a war on any religion or a region; it was a war on a group of evil people who were terrorizing the fabric of the human civilization. If America lost this war, that would mean the end of the civilized world, and there was an overwhelming support for the Iraq war, the guest argued. She turned off the TV as it was too much for her.

Nicole sat in the family room staring at the blank TV. She felt worried, terrified, lost, and depressed and started crying. She did not know how long she had been crying when she was startled by the door bell. She slowly dragged herself out of the sofa seat and started walking towards the door. Her heart was heavy, and she could feel the storms brewing inside her head. It was as if she has a premonition and was expecting some terrible news. Her heart sank when she opened the door and saw a uniformed marine officer. The officer gave her the marine salute and handed over an envelope to her. Tears started flowing on her cheeks as she received the envelope. The man stood there with his head bowed down, not saying a word. After a long silence, he looked up and apologized with utmost sincerity.

"I am terribly sorry, Ma'am," the officer uttered. He knew exactly how Nicole felt and what was going on through her mind. This was not the first time he had to do the most unpleasant part of his job. He then turned back and started walking towards his vehicle.

Nicole slowly closed the door and walked back to the family room and opened the letter. She could not read the whole letter, but she knew that Junior was gone, killed by a roadside bomber. She screamed and cried incessantly and refused to accept the truth. She felt uncontrollable convulsions in her body as she fell on the sofa. She cried for ten minutes before she was overtaken by anger and rage. Engulfed by uncontrollable emotions, she rushed to the backyard and started throwing the garden furniture into the pool until she was too exhausted to continue. She sat there, confused, not sure what to do next.

What if they are wrong? Maybe they had incorrect information. Perhaps, Junior is lost somewhere in the Iraqi desert, she reasoned. The thought of Junior being lost and alone in an inhospitable desert terrified her. She had to do something about it. It was her duty to go to Iraq and find him. She did not want to waste even a single minute. *I hate these bureaucrats, they never do anything right,* she murmured to herself.

She grabbed her passport and purse and packed a minimal amount of personal items into a carry-on and rushed to her car. As she got out of the garage, she quickly closed the garage door and started speeding towards the "Big" Airport on the turnpike.

Chapter 9
Family Secret

Johan got out of his last class at 2:40 PM. He had signed up for off-campus physical education which allowed him to skip the last hour of school and attend rigorous tennis training at a nearby tennis academy. It was the last semester of his junior high school, and in the fall he was going to start attending senior high school. In a few months, the school would be over, and Johan was looking forward for an intense tournament season during the summer. As he walked towards the front of the school, the mild spring breeze kept ruffling his wavy hair. He got a little anxious as he failed to locate his mom's SUV. Why was she late today, he wondered. He was struck with a mild sense of worry as she was always the one in front of the carpool lane.

He walked towards a tree nearby, took out his cell phone and dialed Nicole's number. To his chagrin, the phone kept ringing until it went to her voicemail. Irritated, he ended the call without leaving a message; he was going to be late for practice. He was eager for his practice session as he had mentally developed some new serve and volley strategies that he wanted to try out. After five minutes of restless waiting, his irritation morphed into a deeper worry, a fear that her mother might have gotten into an accident. He tried to convince himself that it was an irrational fear and quickly grabbed his phone and dialed his mom again. However, this yielded the same outcome as before. Concerned, he ended his call and immediately called his dad.

"Hi, Dad, this is Johan," he sounded extremely anxious as John answered the call.

"Hi, Johan, What is going on, you sound very worried. Is Mom with you?"

"No. That's why I'm calling you. I tried to call her twice, but I get no answer," Johan explained.

"She's probably stuck in traffic where the coverage is bad; don't worry, she will be there in few minutes" John tried to assure his son. However, deep inside he was worried as he was the only one who knew Nicole's true condition.

"Dad, there is no traffic at this hour. I am really worried. Can you come and pick me up?" Johan pleaded. He had forgotten all about his practice and his immediate concern was the well being of his mother.

"All right, I will be there in ten minutes," John assured his son and was immediately on his way to meet Johan.

As soon as Johan saw his dad's car approaching the school, he rushed to the curb to wait for him to stop the car. In a second he was inside the car urging his dad to speed up.

"Dad, let's hurry, I am worried about Mom. Maybe something bad happened to her," Johan sounded distraught.

"John, let us not jump to any conclusions. She will be all right. Maybe she went shopping and lost track of time," John said, trying to calm Johan down.

John was worried as well as he had tried to reach her several times after he had left his office, each time getting her voice mail. He had also called Dr. Hamilton's office to see if she had visited them but found out that they had never heard from her that day.

When they were close to home, Johan leaned over and pressed the garage door opener, and as the door retreated upwards, exposing an empty garage, his heart sank. He was now scared, and he started trembling. Tears started rolling over his cheeks, and he wondered why he was being so pessimistic about the situation.

John parked the car, turned off the engine, and then put his arm around Johan as he tried to console him. They both got out of the car and as they entered the kitchen area from the attached garage, the first thing they noticed was that the door to the back yard was not locked. They immediately went into the backyard to see if there was anything suspicious. The only thing they noticed was that the yard furniture was trashed all over the backyard, some against the fence, some right in the middle of the lush green lawn, and some in the flower bed.

Was there an intruder? Johan was worried, but John knew better.

They both went back into the house looking for any signs of Nicole. Johan noticed the cell phone on the sofa and immediately brought it to his dad.

"Was there a break-in Dad?"

John looked around and saw that none of the furniture or electronic equipment was touched.

"I do not think so, Johan. Nevertheless, I will call the police to get their help," John replied as he started scrolling down the call log in Nicole's cell phone.

"There is nothing unusual in her call log here," John replied. He then called 911.

Within a few minutes, there was a knock on the front door, and John let the officer in. The officer, introducing himself as officer Rogers, asked John several questions as he periodically took notes. He went from room to room to see if there was any evidence of a break-in. He was very professional in his demeanor and at the end, he gave his assessment.

"After going over all the physical evidence, I do not think that it is a burglary. However, it could be a kidnap or carjacking. I will file this as a potential kidnapping for the time being. If your wife does not come back within the next twenty four hours, we will file this as a missing person," the officer explained the procedure to John as Johan just stood there listening to the briefing.

"Do you have a digital picture of your wife I can upload it to the police system? That will help us track your wife," the officer added.

John nodded his head and quickly went into his study while Johan sat on a chair, head down, not knowing what to do next. Within a few minutes, John came back with a USB flash drive that contained a few of Nicole's recent pictures and handed over to the officer.

After the officer had left and John had closed the front door, Johan came to his dad and hugged him. He stayed there in that position for a long time and slowly whispered his desperation.

"I'm scared, Dad. Will we ever find mom?"

"We will, we will Johan. Let's go and visit all the places she frequented and see if we will locate her," John assured his son.

Over the next four hours, they visited all the places that Nicole frequented including the grocery store, the meditation hall, the tennis center, and the Bob Woodruff Park east of US 75. They found no trace of either Nicole or her car in any of these places. The last place to check on John's list was Dr. Hamilton's office. Although he had called their office and verified that she had not visited them that afternoon, he still had a nagging feeling that she might have gone into that area. Perhaps she had gone to the office and parked her car in a nearby street and never got out of the car. John knew how much she resented visiting the doctor's office. That was a constant remainder to her that everything was not all right in her head, something that only bothered her.

When John and Johan arrived at the building that housed the doctor's office, the parking lot was empty as all the offices in the building were closed. They decided to drive around the area to look for Nicole's car; unfortunately, there were no signs of her car anywhere in the neighborhood. Frustrated, John decided to head back home.

After they reached home, John sat on the sofa in the family room contemplating what he should do next. Was Nicole kidnapped? Did she leave on her own? If that were true, he knew exactly what had prompted her to resort to such a course. There was never a day or night when he did not worry about her illness.

"Dad, shouldn't we be calling the police officer to see if they have found anything about mom?" Johan prompted his dad realizing that he was somewhat overwhelmed and lost. John agreed as he nodded his head and took his cell phone out to call Officer Rogers. Once he was connected to the officer, he asked if they had found any leads or information about Nicole.

"I am sorry, Mr. Watts, we have not been able to find any new information or lead. We are still looking for your wife's car. We have sent her car license number to all the police departments in the Metroplex," the officer replied.

"We will definitely contact you as soon as we have any new lead or information," the officer assured John.

That did not comfort Johan who was sitting close to his dad to listen to the conversation as he leaned against his dad looking for some solace. There was a prolonged silence as they both sat motionless for a long time.

"Why don't you go and fix yourself some dinner. I will go and check Nicole's email account to see if there is anything there that can give us a lead," advised John as he stood up and walked into the study.

For the next several hours, he went through the email account and searched her folders to uncover any possible leads to solve the mystery. It was almost midnight when he was done with his search. He felt exhausted and decided to take a break and lay down on the sofa. He could hardly rest as his mind wandered endlessly from the time he had met Nicole in Paris to the afternoon when he got a desperate call from Johan. He was aware of all the issues Nicole had with her mental health and Dr. Hamilton had cautioned him several times about potential irrational reactions by her. Nevertheless, John had a faith that their love was strong enough to overcome any irrational urge caused by a chemical imbalance in her brain. He got emotional as he realized that he should had been more careful and taken some extra precautions. He had to find her, his heart and soul was not in any position to bear another tragedy. He silently cried as his mind wandered to the day when his parents were drowned by the flash flood in Lubbock.

After a lot of hard work and perseverance, his business efforts had paid off handsomely. His company was making good money and he had even received buy out offers from larger companies that were entrenched in the oil business. The offers were so large that they had even shocked John; it did not totally surprise him however as the demand for oil was skyrocketing and there seemed to be no end to the oil services business boom. He was yet to accept any of those offers, and the idea that Nicole might not be there to enjoy the fruits of his hard work and business success made him uncontrollably sick.

John had fallen asleep when he was woken by the loud ringing of his cell phone. He looked at the name display and came to a heightened state of awareness as he realized that it was officer Rogers on the other end of the call.

"Mr. Watts, we have located your wife's car. It was parked in the DFW airport parking lot," the officer explained. Before John could say anything, he gave him a small task. "Can you check your credit cards and see if you wife bought any airline ticket in the last twenty four hours?"

John kept the officer on hold and quickly logged into his American Express account to see the latest transactions, and when he did not find any latest transaction, he decided to call the customer service.

"Let me contact American Express and I will call you back later," John promised the officer as he ended the call.

The representative at American Express was indeed very helpful and searched his account for latest charges that were yet to be posted online. She found one transaction that had a time stamp of 4:30 PM. It was an American Airline ticket from Dallas to London.

John now realized that the situation was out of reach of local law enforcement agencies as Nicole's disappearance did not appear to be a case of a missing person. Nor did it look like a case of kidnapping as there was no evidence physical or otherwise to indicate that. John had to now take it upon himself to find his wife. He immediately hired a private detective agency that had experience in dealing with disappearances across international borders to search for Nicole, and committed more than one hundred thousand dollars to find Nicole. Money was no issue for him as he loved his wife beyond limits and was willing to spend as much money as required to locate her, even if it meant spending millions of dollars.

The one who was devastated the most from Nicole's appearance was indeed Johan as it had turned his life upside down. His whole life including, his tennis career was now on hold.

A few days had passed since Nicole's disappearance as Johan and John sat at the kitchen table getting ready for a quick dinner. They had ordered pizza as neither of them was in any mood for a real meal.

Johan looked at his dad who looked tired and dazed. He noticed circles around his eyes from sleepless nights and there were more lines on his forehead, and it was as if he had aged ten years in the past few days. He hated himself for raising the question of his mom's health, but he could no longer hold it inside as the pain had become intolerable.

"What exactly was wrong with Mom, Dad?" Johan asked the question knowing it was going to cause more heartache for his dad. He had to ask him as he wanted to understand the whole situation; he even felt that he was entitled to an answer as he was no longer a kid. He felt like he had aged several years just in the last few days. John felt the same way too; he himself had come to a conclusion that Johan should be told the whole story.

John looked at Johan's face, a face that had altered unimaginably over the last few days. He no longer had that innocent teenager look; rather it was the look of a youth who was determined to find out about his roots. Johan was not bothered whether his question would take time as he felt that not knowing about his mother's situation was like not knowing about his own past. He knew it was time for him to face up to the truth, however cruel the answer might be.

John slowly started unveiling the secret he had meticulously hid from Johan until now. He told Johan about the accident Nicole's parents had when she was a little girl. It was a fatal car crash that had killed both her parents. That accident had played havoc on little Nicole's mind and she had become schizophrenic. She often exhibited multiple personalities and would at times have nightmares that made her scream throughout the night. Her aunt who had raised her did her best to seek help. She had tried everything from traditional medicine to non-traditional methods such as hypnosis and martial arts technique. Nothing seemed to work until she enrolled Nicole in a mediation class at a Buddhist center. That had helped Nicole enormously and over months her nightmares had stopped. Meditation coupled with classes about Buddha's teachings she attended changed her life completely. Over the next few years, her schizophrenic behavior had completely stopped, and she had become a devout follower of the Enlightened One.

"I thought that mom's parents died of some rare tropical disease they contacted when they were visiting Africa," Johan interrupted the story.

"That was just a fake story we made up to protect you," John replied as he continued with the story.

Nicole was aware of her condition when she met John and had told the details to him. That did not stop John from marrying her. Indeed, their happy marriage helped strengthen her mental condition and everything seemed to be on a positive trajectory until that fateful night.

It was a few years after John and Nicole were married and Nicole was pregnant with their first child. A few months into the pregnancy, Nicole had severe abdominal pain and John had rushed her to the nearest hospital. Although the doctors attended to her immediately, the unthinkable had happened, and the pregnancy had ended in a miscarriage.

For the next few months, John saw Nicole develop multiple personalities. She was at times hysteric throwing things at him. At times, she would be like a child sitting in a corner sobbing continuously. She would periodically point at something and her sobbing would intensify; it was as if she was pointing towards a road accident. There were days when she would be completely hostile towards John. She would give him the silent treatment and frown at him whenever he came near her. There were times she would treat John like a little boy. In this phase, she would assume the role of a teacher and John would be her favorite student. None of this terrified John or made him lose his patience. John now knew exactly what she meant by her unknown mental condition before they were married. One of the syndromes she had developed in her mind was that she never had a miscarriage and had a healthy boy whom she had named "Junior" in her mind.

John had consulted many mental health specialists seeking help but none of the doctors he had visited had made progress in treating her until he took her to Dr. Hamilton. Dr. Hamilton used a combination of traditional technique mixed with many non-traditional methods like meditation to help his parents which started to have a positive impact on Nicole. Over a period of one year she was back to being normal except for occasional mood swings that always involved Junior.

"I knew Junior was not real, Dad. I figured that out several years ago," Johan stated. The whole story had made him sad. He wished that he was more understanding towards his mother; if only he had known her condition. Noticing Johan was saddened by his narration, John put his arms around his shoulders trying to comfort him. They both sat silently at the kitchen table for a long time trying to gather enough strength to say anything.

"Dad, I have a secret to confess," Johan whispered trying to break the silence.

"What is it, Johan?"

Before Johan could reply, John felt the vision; the terrifying scenes from a medieval war, and he was thrown into the battle filed where warriors were in a killing binge. The mindless massacre of innocent monks continued as blood spilled all over the grounds. Buildings were burning, creating a scene more terrifying than any hell he had ever imagined.

John started sweating profusely and withdrew his hand from Johan. He was so terrified from that vision he was practically shaking. Johan knew that his own dad had now experienced his vision that no longer frightened him.

"What does it all mean, Dad?" Johan wanted to know if his dad could make any sense of his vision.

John, who had recovered by now, nodded his head sideways indicating he did know the answer. After a brief time, he replied, "Perhaps it is something about your past life. It is almost like something I had read a long time ago in a Jataka[8] story."

---

8 *Jataka stories are a branch of Buddhist literature native to India concerning the previous births of the Buddha.*

CHAPTER 10
Adjusting to A New Life

J ohan was lonely like never before, and he felt completely
lost. He was like a child lost in a dark forest, looking for
his bearings. He was angry and confused; confused about
the conflicting feelings that engulfed him every minute
of his life. There was even a feeling of guilt - guilt that
he should have been a better child so that he could have
somehow helped his mother. He had trouble focusing on
anything and everything he did from school to tennis and
felt like a drifter. He even wondered about the intricacies of
the human mind and was saddened that past events could
have such a devastating impact on one's psyche. Memory is
a bad thing, he concluded. It is memory that causes hatred
and warfare, he had reasoned. That thought stayed with him
for just a fraction of second when he realized that he was
being irrational, which terrified him as it made him wonder
if he was going crazy.

If only we knew how the human brain cells are arranged,
and if only we could fix any dislocations in that structure
like engineers fix electronic circuits, would that not be
marvelous - his wandering mind refused to stop thinking.
If only if it was that simple, how nice it would be for those
who are suffering from mental illness, he lamented.

John, despite his own emotional struggles, was acutely aware of Johan's condition. He wanted to make sure that the tragic event would not scar Johan's young mind permanently and tried to provide as much emotional support as possible. He made sure that he spent as much time as possible with Johan, from his school work to tennis practice, despite his overwhelmingly busy schedule. At the same time, he kept working with the private investigators to track down Nicole. He kept tracking her movements through her credit card usage; he had not cancelled the card just so that they could track her movement. The last transaction they had tracked was in Rome, Italy, and after that there was no more transaction for almost a month. One day all of a sudden, there was an ATM transaction in Cairo, Egypt that appeared on the bank account. That was the last transaction he saw and everything stopped after that. John had investigators visit Rome and Cairo, but they had come out empty with no trace of Nicole.

John had been always close to Johan, and the tragic event brought them even closer. However, it was difficult for John to run his business and be a full time father to Johan at the same time which pained him a lot. John did not want Johan to be depressed all the time, and he kept thinking about ways to get him out of his deep melancholic state.

"Johan, now that you are sixteen, I want you to enroll in the driving school, and get your driving license." John brought up the topic during a breakfast.

"That is a good idea, Dad. That way you don't have to give me ride every time I have to go somewhere." Johan was somewhat pleased with that suggestion.

He had wondered about the SUV that was sitting idle in the garage, but he was too depressed to say anything about it.

The driving school helped Johan forget about his misery a little, but he was still a depressed teenager. He was so depressed that each night he went to bed hoping that the yogi would come to him in his dreams; it was a simple expectation that the yogi would give him some words of wisdom that would calm his mind and help him spring back to his normal self. Unfortunately, that expectation never materialized, making him even more melancholic. As time went by, that simple expectation became a desperate hope, a cry for help.

He had almost given up his hope of communing with the guru, when one day in his sleep, the yogi appeared. This time, however, it happened differently and Johan found himself on the top of a mountain peak where he could see his yogi meditating. The mountain peak was covered with light mist as he slowly started walking towards his guru, and when he reached the yogi, he was still meditating. Johan stood in front of the yogi waiting for him to open his eyes; the wait was no more than five minutes, yet it felt like eternity to young Johan. The yogi finally opened his eyes and addressed Johan.

"Please come and sit in front of me, Johan. I know you are very sad about your mother's disappearance. I am sorry to see you in this depressed state," Yogi addressed Johan.

The moment he heard those words, Johan started crying uncontrollably.

"Will I see my mother again, Yogi?" he asked while he continued to sob.

"You will, Johan, you will. But that may take a long time, and you need to come back to your previous self," the yogi advised.

"But Yogi, how do I get out this state?"

"You need to stop worrying too much about the past. You can't change the past. All you can do is to get acclimated to the current life. You need to make adjustments, and that is all you can do."

Johan sat quietly in front of the yogi, trying to comprehend yogi's advice.

"One more thing I want to tell you, Johan. This is the last time we meet like this. The next time we see each other, it is going to be in person," the yogi added as he slowly disappeared into the mist which woke up Johan.

Johan sat up on his bed trying to understand what the yogi had said in his dream. Make adjustments, is that all he could advise me? Johan felt a bit disappointed and as his disappointment grew, he even felt betrayed. There was a feeling of let down by his master, and he felt deeply hurt. He laid on his back staring at the ceiling wondering why the yogi would not help him and trying to see if there was a deeper meaning in Yogi's advice. He was staring at the ceiling so long that it started looking like an endless tunnel which helped him focus on the true meaning of his guru's advice. The more he thought about that advice, the more it became clearer, and he had to agree with the yogi. The yogi was right; the only thing he could do was to make the adjustments. He surely could not change the past, but he could influence the future, and the only way he could do that was by making proper adjustments. He felt relieved and even happier and promised the yogi that he was going to do just that.

In the next few months, Johan had his provisional Texas driving license, which along with his mom's car added a whole new dimension to his life. He could now visit Nick anytime he wanted, and he started practicing tennis with Nick as often as possible. During and after tennis sessions, they would chat about school, tournaments, the pro-circuit, and got closer to each other. During a practice session, Johan brought up their future college plans.

"What do you want to major in when you go to college, Nick?"

"I know exactly what I want to study. I want to study psychology. The human mind is something that fascinates me a lot," replied Nick. "What about you?"

"I don't know. Maybe literature or maybe engineering like my dad. I haven't really made up my mind. So, have you read about psychology, Nick?" Johan became inquisitive.

Nick nodded his head with a big smile. "More than I should be reading at this stage. From Freud to Jung and even some declassified CIA documents," Nick laughed as he explained his interest in CIA documents.

Nick's interest in psychology had piqued Johan's curiosity. Can psychology really help understand human mind? Perhaps he should mention Nick about his childhood visions and see his reaction, Johan mused.

"Can I tell you something I have never shared with anyone other than my dad?"

"If you want to, Johan; don't tell me if you aren't comfortable with it."

"I want to tell you. It is a very strange and scary vision, and you may not believe me."

As Johan explained his childhood vision, Nick listened intently without interruption. He became very curious and fascinated, and his level of curiosity increased several folds when Johan mentioned his interactions with the yogi in his dreams.

"I am sure that there are some explanations to your dreams and visions, Johan. That will be the first topic for my future research," Nick joked.

"Maybe, Nick; but deep inside I feel like it is something from my past life."

Nick knew that Johan was raised in the Buddhist tradition, and he wondered if his dreams were influenced by the stories he had heard as a child, but he did not say anything about it. He knew very well that religion could be a sensitive topic even among friends. For some strange reason, sharing his secret with Nick only made their bond of friendship stronger than ever.

The months passed by, and Johan had indeed made adjustments to his new life. He was now a senior and was looking forward to his college career. He and Nick had selected the same colleges; UT, Texas A&M, Harvard, Princeton, and Stanford. They had prepared for the college entrance tests together and had decided to go to the same college and room together in the dorm. Tennis had now taken a secondary role and they participated in a minimal number of tournaments.

However, Johan's dwindling interest in tennis was a big disappointment for his sponsor, especially Reggie Walker, the agent. Indeed, he had made several trips to Plano to meet with Johan and John. He had tried his best to encourage Johan to take part in national level tournaments hoping national level competition would reignite his competitive spirits. Unfortunately for Johan, his inability to connect with the yogi had eroded his mental focus, and he could no longer play at the level that had made him a tennis prodigy. He had resigned to that fact and his dream of becoming a tennis professional had slowly dissipated.

It was during that transitory period, Johan had discovered classic rock music. He had one day found his dad's music collection and started listening to the bands that were popular in the seventies and eighties, and soon he was hooked to classic rock. The Beatles, The Doors, The Bad Company, AC/DC, The Eagles and so on - they all had become his favorite bands. He had downloaded the old songs into his iPod and his computer, and those songs had a therapeutic power that made him forget about his misery.

John on the other hand could never make the adjustments to a life without Nicole. While his business was booming beyond his wildest dreams, he felt utterly empty inside. He never gave up on finding Nicole and spent hundreds of thousands of dollars on private investigators to track her. All the leads had eventually dried up and in the end, even the private investigators had given up on the search. John was so distraught at that point that he even considered joining a monastery and becoming a monk. The only thing that kept him going was his love for Johan. Because of his love for Johan, he never showed any of his deep-seated pain outside and kept his agony to himself.

When both Nick and Johan got their acceptance letters from Stanford in early May, they were both ecstatic. As Stanford was their first choice, they immediately accepted the offer and did not bother to wait for the decision from other schools.

As the last days of Johan's senior year approached, John made up his mind to sell his business. He decided to buy a private jet and a condo in the San Francisco area so that he could visit Johan as often as possible.

CHAPTER 11
California

The first quarter at Stanford went by really fast, and before Johan and Nick could even settle down in their dorm room, they felt overwhelmed with the course load. Even for brilliant students like Nick and Johan, the tests and quizzes seemed quite difficult. They both found themselves studying late hours on a regular basis and found little time for relaxation. The only relaxation they had was playing tennis together on weekends, and luckily for them they managed to get good marks in all of their courses. They knew that since every student at the school was smart, letter grades were very competitive as the professors graded them on the curve. When the quarter was over, they both breathed a sigh of relief as they had gotten only good grades.

While Johan was more of an introvert and did not seek out friends, Nick was rather gregarious and had already developed friendship with several other kids. One of the students he had met in an advanced psychology course was Kaya, who was a brilliant student of psychology. Nick and Kaya had teamed together in some of the class papers and Kaya often came to the dorm room after studying in the library. Johan had met Kaya a couple of times and nothing extraordinary had occurred between him and Kaya; however, that all changed one day.

It was a Saturday afternoon, and Johan had gone to spend some time with Pranav Kumar Rao, a student he had befriended in his mathematics class. Pranav, nick named PK, was a student from India who was majoring in engineering just like Johan. After they had worked jointly on some difficult math concepts for almost three hours, they decided to take a break and walked towards a coffee shop that was just outside the campus. As they entered the coffee shop, they ran into Nick and Kaya, and Nick greeted them to join at the table, and introduced Kaya to PK as it was the first time they had met each other.

After ordering some coffee, they sat around the table with PK and Johan on one side and Nick and Kaya on the other side. They were talking about a movie they all had seen at different times when the store clerk yelled out that their orders were ready. Johan and Nick walked towards the counter to bring the drinks; Johan carried Kaya's coffee and brought it to her. As he handed over the coffee cup to her, he inadvertently touched her hand, and something extraordinary happened at that moment. Johan had a vision - a vision that was unbelievably pleasant, and it was nothing like the scary battlefield visions he used to have as a child. There were no battle cries with streams of blood or monks being beheaded, and instead he was in a beautiful garden near a pristine pond, and he heard some melodious albeit exotic music. It seemed so real and intoxicating that Johan wanted to freeze time, but it was all gone in just few seconds as he tried to regain his composure and get his bearings back. He looked up at Kaya's green eyes trying to guess if she had sensed anything extraordinary. She gave him no indication of what had transpired on her side, but she indeed had sensed a strange feeling as well. It was not a vision; it was rather a feeling like she had known Johan all her life. It puzzled her beyond limits as it was a feeling one gets when they meet someone very close after a long painful separation. Only in this case she felt like she knew Johan from her past life and she had been separated from him for hundreds of years. It was all the more puzzling to her since it was not the first time she had met Johan, but she tried to shake off that strange feeling and pretended to be immersed in the conversation around the table.

Several days had passed since that strange encounter with Kaya, and Johan tried to brush off the event as something non-consequential to him. However, Johan could never stop thinking about that afternoon at the coffee house which baffled him endlessly. Soon, the afternoon event had engulfed his whole head, and he knew that he had to do something about it. He had to get to know Kaya to find out why he had that strange yet enormously pleasing vision that afternoon. He was puzzled; he was intrigued and even bewildered. Was their some sort of connection between this new vision and the visions he used to have as a child?

A few days later, after they had completed dinner, Johan decided to ask Nick for Kaya's number.

"Nick, do you have Kaya's cell phone number?"

Nick was somewhat surprised by that as he had assumed that there was no spark whatsoever between Kaya and Johan. At least, that was his initial analysis.

"I do. What's going on?" Nick replied.

"I'll explain later. I need to find out more about her. I have to – otherwise I'll go crazy."

"OK. No pressure. Let me know how it goes."

Nick gave Kaya's number to Johan and walked out of the room to the library. Johan sat on his bed and quickly composed a message to Kaya.

"Hi, Kaya, this is Johan."

Kaya was not entirely surprised when her phone beeped and she saw that message.

"Hi, Johan, how are you?" was her polite reply.

Johan texted back, "Can I call you?"

"Sure," Kaya replied.

Within a minute, Kaya's phone rang, and she answered.

"Hi, Johan. Is everything all right?"

"Yes. Everything is fine. I want to explain something I experienced in the coffee house the other day," Johan began awkwardly.

Indeed, Kaya herself had wondered about the strange feeling she had that day and was more than curious to explore that topic. Nevertheless, she pretended to be ignorant of what was in Johan's mind.

"What are you talking about?"

"It's hard to explain on the phone. Can we meet at the coffee shop? Perhaps we can discuss it in private," Johan replied.

It seemed like a simple request and Kaya was agreeable to it. "That is fine with me. I will meet you there in ten minutes."

As soon as he had ended the call, Johan started walking briskly towards the coffee shop. He had to discover more about Kaya, and he was now more than convinced that there was somehow a mysterious connection between his childhood visions and Kaya. What is that connection, he wondered. What if this new added dimension made his life more complicated; there never seemed to be a limit for twists and turns in his young life. He was worried for a minute but quickly realized that not finding the answers was not an option. It was certainly not an option when it comes to matters of heart and wherever it took him, he was ready to face it; he was ready for the future even if it meant learning about his past.

CHAPTER 12
Kaya

Kaya and Johan sat around a small round table sipping coffee. Johan had come earlier and had ordered two coffees, and Kaya had joined him shortly after that. She too was very curious about what had happened the last time they were in the coffee shop, and she had come to join Johan as fast as she could.

"I feel somewhat silly. I don't know where to begin," Johan started the conversation.

"That is all right. You can tell me anything, and I won't discuss it with anyone else," Kaya assured. She sensed that Johan was somewhat anxious and even a little bit nervous.

"I sometimes see things. You may call them visions. Strange visions – they are very hard for me to explain."

Fortunately for Johan, Kaya did not laugh or make fun of his statement; nor did she patronize him. She did not see anything unusual with that statement, perhaps because she was a psychology major or perhaps because of her Native American heritage.

"Can you give me some details? I don't know if I can help you in anyway though."

Johan sipped some coffee and tried to get his thoughts together. He did not know how to begin.

"You don't think that I am crazy or some sort of nut?"

"Don't be silly. People experience all sorts of super natural things. Some can be explained by science and many are still unresolved mysteries." Kaya's response put him a little at ease.

"I have had these visions from the time I was a child. Some of them are very scary," Johan explained.

"You get them regularly?"

"No, they are somewhat random. However, for the past few years they have stopped. But something strange happened the last time we were here. That is why I wanted to meet you here."

Johan looked into Kaya's eyes to sense if she had experienced anything similar that day. This time Kaya's eyes were not hiding anything and it was obvious to Johan that she had indeed experienced something special.

"When I touched your hand, I was instantly transported to a palace in an exotic world near a garden and a pristine pond. There was a palace, the palace and the garden were beautiful and there were swans and lilies in the pond. I also heard melodious music, and it all seemed like something from an ancient time from a faraway place. But the vision lasted for a short while, perhaps, a few seconds and it was all gone," Johan explained.

Kaya listened to him intently, and she clearly had a puzzled look as she listened to his narration.

"I want to reveal this to you, Johan. It was a strange feeling as well for me; I did hear some exotic music, but I had no visions. Like you said, it lasted for only a few seconds." Kaya tried to make some sense out of her experience the other day.

Johan felt unbelievably happy when he heard that and indeed he could sense a special connection. Having established that they both had experienced a special feeling the last time they were there, he wanted to explore it even further. He gazed deep into her green eyes and slowly held her hands as he focused on her face. As he held her hands that were unbelievably soft, he felt a surge of electricity go through his entire body. Soon, everything around them became dark, and he was no longer in the coffee shop. They were transported into a different realm – the same exotic palace he had seen a few days ago. There was the same beautiful garden near the pristine pond with floating swans, and he could hear the same exotic music. This time he was not alone. There was Kaya standing next to him dressed like a princess. It all seemed real, but he knew it was only a vision. The most pleasing part of that experience was that Johan felt unbelievably happy, and he looked at Kaya again. The mild breeze made her wavy hair dance in front of her eyes, and he slowly moved his hand to hold her face. Suddenly, it was all gone, and he was again staring at Kaya's face in the coffee shop. This time Kaya had closed her eyes, and he sensed that she was perspiring in her hands.

"Did you see anything?" Johan whispered.

"Yes, I did, I saw what you had described earlier," Kaya sounded shaken a bit.

"You saw the pond, the swans, and the palace?"

"Yes, I did. The strange thing is you were there dressed like a prince. I do not know what it all means," Kaya replied, sounding concerned.

"Let's go back to the campus. This is more than I can handle in one evening," Kaya got up and wanted Johan to walk with her back to the campus.

That night, neither Johan nor Kaya could sleep very well. They had both realized that they were deeply in love with each other. It did not feel like a man and a woman falling in love for the first time, but it felt as if they were two lovers finding each other after a long separation.

Soon it became obvious to everyone that they were in love. Nick was happy and thought that Johan and Kaya were made for each other. However, when Johan explained to him about the new vision he had started having, he got a little concerned. It was not that he did not believe in Johan's story; he was concerned that Johan's strange visions were taking on a life of their own and that soon Johan's life would be swept up by these strange visions.

It was now almost a week since Johan and Kaya had discovered their mysterious connection. The coffee shop had now become their favorite spot, and they visited that place almost daily.

"Johan, I want you to visit my ancestral reservation and meet my grandma," Kaya announced abruptly.

"Sure, where is your reservation?"

"It's in Arizona. It is a few hundred miles North-West of Phoenix."

"When do you want us to go there?"

"Can we go this weekend?" Kaya sounded anxious to make the trip. She wanted Johan to meet her grandmother as she was convinced that her grandma would shed some light on the mysterious connection between herself and Johan.

"Sorry, Kaya, not this weekend. My dad is going to be here, and he is taking me to see the ATP tournament at Indian Wells."

Kaya kept quiet and did not say anything.

"Would you like to join us? My dad will not mind," Johan added.

"No, you go ahead and have a good time with your dad. I don't want to come between you and your dad. Can we visit my grandma the weekend after that?"

"Sure, you seem to be anxious. Should be fun," Johan replied with a smile.

The next weekend, Johan and his dad flew to Palm Springs to attend the tennis tournament. John had bought the weekend package for the two of them as he wanted to spend some quality time with his son. John had just returned from a business trip to Indonesia and looked relaxed. Ever since he had sold his company, John did occasional consulting work with the large corporation that had bought his company. They had paid so much money for his company that there was no need for him to work any more. Nevertheless, he did the consulting work to keep himself challenged intellectually.

That weekend turned out to be very pleasant, and Johan was glad that he had a chance to spend time with his dad. He was a little disappointed that neither Federer nor Nadal made into the finals. Nevertheless, he enjoyed the tournament and felt reenergized. His father flew him back to Stanford, and later that week, John flew back to Dallas.

One week after that, Johan and Kaya flew to Phoenix. They rented an SUV, and Kaya drove towards the reservation.

Kaya's grandmother, who had spent most of her life on the reservation, was the first woman from her tribe to go to college. She had studied archeology at UC Berkeley and had planned to do a doctoral degree. After finishing her undergraduate studies, she had travelled to Peru to work with an archeology expedition team. That is where she had met her husband, another archeologist from Europe, and Kaya's mother was born in Peru. Soon after that, Kaya's grandfather had died after contracting a rare tropical disease. Her grandma had then moved back to the reservation and had raised Kaya's mother.

Kaya never talked about her parents, and Johan never pushed her on that topic. From the way Kaya had talked about her grandma, Johan knew that they had a special relationship. As Kaya drove the SUV along the rural Arizona road, Johan noticed that the breeze was mild and the scenery was exquisite. The red rock formations and the desert vegetation added an air of mystery to the whole journey. After a few hours of journey, they were getting close to the reservation and Johan could see a group of adobe structures not too far away.

As they entered the reservation, Kaya stopped their vehicle and started walking towards two children who were running towards her. As they got closer, she ran and hugged the children and brought them to the SUV. The children sat in the back seat and were excited to see Kaya. At the same time, they seemed very curious about Johan as very few outsiders came and visited the reservation. Kaya drove the car for few hundred yards and stopped the car in front of one of the larger adobe houses. As she and the kids got down, an older woman came out rushing and hugged Kaya, and they stayed in that position for a long time. The two kids ran into another adobe house shouting, "Kaya is here!"

Johan slowly walked towards the two of them, and when Kaya finally separated from her grandmother, she introduced Johan.

"This is Johan, Grandma; Grandma, this is Johan I mentioned over the phone." She felt weird not knowing why she was repeating herself.

"Hello, Johan. I am so happy to meet you. Kaya has talked a lot about you. Welcome to our home," she gave him a warm welcome. Her smile and welcome was so genuine that Johan instantly felt comfortable even though the surroundings seemed strange to him.

Kaya and grandma kept talking for a while with Johan sitting in the room as an observer. He got up and walked around the house looking at the art that was hung on the walls. Everything seemed different to Johan and soon he started smelling some exotic aroma coming from the kitchen. He realized that dinner was being served as grandma went inside the kitchen and brought out some plates to set the table.

The dinner was all vegetarian as Kaya has informed her grandma that Johan was a vegetarian. After dinner was over, Kaya excused herself and went to the next house which gave an opportunity for grandma to spend time with Johan alone. Her name was Angel, and she asked him about general things like his school and reading interests. Often, she would hold his hands and feel them as if she was trying to find the real Johan. At one point, she took his right palm and started reading the lines.

"Can you read my palm?" Johan quizzed.

"Of course I can. This something I learned when I was in Peru."

"Did you learn that from the native people of Peru?"

"No, my late husband taught me."

"What do you see, Grandma?" Johan was curious.

"Your life is going to take an unexpected turn. It is like you are in this world to complete an unfinished mission," she replied.

By that time, Kaya came back to the house and Angel did not elaborate any further on her reading. Johan did not put much credence to what Angel said although he always felt that there was a mysterious mission that was waiting for him.

The next morning, soon after breakfast, Johan and Kaya left the reservation and drove back to Phoenix. This time, Johan decided to drive, and as they drove along the scenic roadway, he wanted to know what Angel had told Kaya about him.

"What did your grandma think of us as a couple?" Johan brought up the topic.

"I told her about your visions and what we had experienced together. She is convinced that our lives are a continuation of where we had left off in our past life."

"She thinks that we were together in past life?"

"Yes, she does. She is a believer in reincarnation of souls."

"Where did she learn about reincarnation?"

"She learnt it from my grandfather. Before coming to Peru, my grand father had lived in India and had spent several years with Hindu mystics."

Johan was really concerned about what Kaya's grandmother had told him the previous night. He wondered what she meant by his life taking an unexpected turn in the near future; he hoped that whatever it was, it was for the better. He had seen too many unpleasant turns in his young life, and he was not ready for another major change in his life.

CHAPTER 13
Johan's Tragedy

The next few weeks went by quickly for Johan and Kaya. The projects, the exams, and term papers kept them extremely busy, and when the quarter was finally over, they were both relieved and looked forward to a more relaxing summer. Johan had gotten an internship in a small startup company in San Jose. He was looking forward to that while Nick, Kaya, and PK had all decided to enroll in some summer courses at Stanford. Nick and Johan were planning to go back to Dallas and spend a week with their families before coming back to Stanford. Kaya had already gone back to the Reservation to be with her grandmother while PK was going to spend a week with some friends in Southern California.

Meanwhile, Johan's dad had returned to Dallas from his second trip to Indonesia. His plan was to fly his plane to San Jose and fly Nick and Johan back to Dallas. Both Nick and Johan were done with their exams on Tuesday and John was scheduled to pick them up on Thursday. This left Wednesday free for them to relax and spend some time with their friends before they flew back to Dallas. Unfortunately, their plans were a bit upset as unexpected storms moved into the Bay area on that Wednesday.

It was late Wednesday and Johan sat on his bed listening to some old music playing on his iPod while Nick sat in another corner reading a book. They were done with their packing and hoped that the bad weather would not upset John's flight plans. The rain kept pounding the dorm window, and the trees outside swayed uncontrollably due to unrelenting gale force wind. The song on the iPod was *Roadside Blues* by *The Doors* and as he listened to the song, he felt sad to the extent that he even felt uncomfortable. The lyric that troubled him went like this: *The future is uncertain and the end is always near.* A few years after composing the song, Morrison had died in Paris the reason being a mystery to his fans even to this day. Johan wondered if Morrison had some sort of premonition about that, and just at that time, his cell phone rang. He stopped the music and picked up the phone and saw that it was Nick's dad on the other end. He wondered why Dr. Hamilton was calling him and hoped that everyone was all right in Dallas. He picked up his phone and answered hesitatingly.

"Hello, this is Johan."

"Johan, this is Dr. Hamilton. Do you have few minutes to talk?"

"Of course, I do. Is everything all right?" Johan sounded worried. He had a good reason to be worried because Dr. Hamilton had never called him on his cell before.

"You father is not feeling well and he will not be able to come to fly you and Nick back to Dallas." He paused for a few seconds hesitating what else to say.

"What is wrong with my father? Can you give me more details?" Johan was anxious to the extent that he felt terrified.

"We do not know. He is having a severe stomach pain. We are going to take him to the Plano Medical Center. I have booked a private plane, and I want you and Nick to go to the airport as soon as possible." Dr. Hamilton tried to calm Johan down.

While Johan was talking to Dr. Hamilton, Nick stopped reading his book and looked at Johan, puzzled and wondering why his dad was talking to him. He quickly realized that something was gravely wrong with Johan's dad and closed his book, waiting for Johan to finish his conversation. At that time, Johan took a pencil and paper and started writing down the details of the private jet that Dr. Hamilton had booked for their flight to Dallas. He soon ended his call and sat on his bed with his head down worried immensely.

Nick walked towards Johan and sat next to him. From just the half of the conversation he had followed, he knew that Johan's father was sick.

"Don't worry, Johan, everything will be all right," he tried to comfort as much he could.

"I don't know, Nick. I am worried," Johan replied as he thought about what Kaya's grandma had told him back on the Reservation. He then handed the piece of paper that had their flight details to Nick. Nick promptly called the number that was on the paper to find out when they could leave the Bay area while Johan kept quiet, hoping that his dad would overcome his medical condition.

"I talked to the pilot. He said we should be able to take off whenever there is a break in the rain. He said that the forecast is that the rain will easy in a couple of hours and we should be able to fly," Nick briefed Johan.

He then went online, searched for the nearest cab service company and called for a cab.

Within a few minutes a cab was near the dorm, and they both rushed down to put their luggage in the cab. Soon they were on their route to the airport. Within forty minutes they were at the airport sitting in the private jet that Dr. Hamilton had arranged as the pilot waited for the permission from the control tower for a departure slot.

When the plane finally started taxiing on the runway, Johan was relieved as he knew that they would be at Dallas airport within the next three hours. The tension within him was too much, and he closed his eyes trying to meditate. In a few minutes he fell asleep and did not wake up until the pilot had announced that they had landed at the Addison airport, a small private airport north of Dallas used mainly for private jets. Nick's dad was waiting in his SUV at the airport, and as soon as they came out of the plane, they loaded the luggage into the SUV and started driving towards Plano. All the time, Johan kept quiet as he was overwhelmed with fear and anxiety deep inside his mind. Finally, he garnered some courage and asked Dr. Hamilton about his dad as the SUV speeded north on Dallas North Tollway towards Plano.

"How is my dad doing?"

"He is in the ICU. The doctors are doing their best to understand the situation," Dr. Hamilton replied.

Johan did not like the answer, nor did he feel encouraged from the tone of Dr. Hamilton's voice as he did not sound very optimistic about the situation.

"What is wrong with my dad? Have they diagnosed his condition?"

"They have not diagnosed it hundred percent at this time, Johan. They think that he has some bacterial infection; he might have gotten that from something he ate while he was in Indonesia," Dr. Hamilton replied.

When they reached Plano Medical Center, it was already midnight and there were very few cars in the parking lot. As soon as Dr. Hamilton parked his car, the three of them rushed to the room where John had been admitted. The room was dark and sparsely lit, and John was lying on the bed with several medical devices attached to his body. Johan slowly walked towards his dad and noticed that he was not conscious. Seeing him in that condition overwhelmed him, and he started quietly sobbing as both Nick and Dr. Hamilton came close to him and tried to comfort him by putting their hands on his shoulder.

Johan sat on a chair next to the bed and held his dad's right palm hoping that his presence would somehow energize his dad. He sat in that position for a long time while Nick and his dad went outside to talk to the doctors who were attending to John.

Johan realized that he had dozed off in that position as he felt a mild tug in his palms. He opened his eyes and looked at his dad who had opened his eyes with a faint smile on his face. Johan felt as if his dad was trying to tell him something. He lowered his head trying to hear what is dad was saying, but all he could hear was his dad's slow breathing which disappointed him. He suddenly felt his dad put is palm on his head and affectionately move his fingers through his hair. And all of a sudden the movement stopped and Johan raised his head and saw that his dad had closed his eyes. He realized that John had left this world and started sobbing quietly.

The next few days were the most difficult days for Johan as he had to take part in the funeral rituals. A Buddhist monk helped him perform the rites while Nick's dad helped him the arrangements. Many of John's friends and associates had come to eulogize him, and one common theme in all eulogies was that John was the most perfect human being they had ever met. Johan had no doubt about that; indeed, he knew that his dad was a perfect human being that had attained Nirvana long before he left this world.

Two of the longtime associates of John who had come all the way from Lubbock to the funeral were Mr. Thompson and Mr. Forrester. Mr. Thompson had remained the financial advisor to John ever since John's parents had drowned in the flash flood. Mr. Forrester had continued to give John legal advice whenever he needed, and the two of them took Johan to side after the funeral and spoke to him softly.

"Johan, I know it is not the perfect time to bring this up. But we need to talk to you about your dad's will," Mr. Thompson explained slowly.

Johan did not say anything as he was still struggling to accept that his dad was not there anymore. Yet he did want to know what his dad's wishes were.

"We can come and meet you tomorrow at your house and go over the details," Mr. Forrester suggested. That sounded reasonable to Johan, and he agreed to meet with them the next afternoon.

Just has Johan had finished talking to Mr. Thompson, his cell phone beeped. Johan opened his phone and realized that it was a message from Kaya. He had been trying to contact her ever since he had heard that his dad was sick but had failed to connect with her as she was in her grand mother's place which had no cell phone coverage. She had finally received his messages as she was on her way back to the Bay area and had immediately sent a message to Johan. Johan went to a corner and called her number.

"Johan, are you all right. I am so sorry to hear about what happened to your dad," she expressed.

There was a long pause as Johan tried hard to suppress his emotions. He finally garnered enough strength and spoke softly.

"I guess it is all my karma like my dad used to say. I have to accept it. The scariest thing is I do not how I am going to navigate my life from now on," Johan sounded lost and dejected.

"I know it is difficult, Johan, and whatever I say now is not going to comfort you. I am sorry I could not be there when you were facing the most difficult time in your life," Kaya was apologetic.

"As soon as I reach Phoenix, I am going to change my flight to Dallas," she continued.

For Johan, those were truly comforting words to hear. He was lonely and desperately wanted her by his side.

When Kaya finally arrived at Dallas it was almost midnight. Johan had driven to the airport and was eagerly waiting for her at the arrival area. As soon as she got out of the security area, Johan ran to her and hugged her. He could hardly comprehend the emotions that went through him at that time. He felt like he had arrived at a point in his life where he was to begin his final journey. He was not scared anymore and was even anxious to start his journey together with Kaya. What was even more surprising to him was that he heard that sweet exotic music the same one he had heard the first time he had met Kaya. He slowly held her hands and looked into Kaya's eyes. She immediately knew what was going on in his head and nodded confirming that she had also heard the music.

The next afternoon, as promised, Mr. Thompson and Mr. Forrester came to see Johan early afternoon.

"Can we sit down and discuss your dad's will in a quiet place?" asked Mr. Forrester.

Johan took them to his dad's study where they sat around the desk. Mr. Forrester took out some legal papers from his briefcase, while Mr. Thompson took out some financial statements. Johan sat quietly waiting for them to explain the contents of those papers.

"Johan, you may not know this, but your dad was a very wealthy man," Mr. Thompson started to brief Johan. Johan had suspected that his dad had acquired a considerable amount of wealth since he had sold his business to a large oil exploration company. Nevertheless, he was unaware of the size of his dad's wealth. Mr. Thompson took the financial papers and spread them on the desk so that Johan could read them, and when Johan saw the statement, he was shocked to see the size of his father's estate. He concentrated on the number at the bottom of the statement to make sure that he was not imagining anything. It was not two or three million of dollars; the total asset value at the bottom of the statement exceeded one hundred million dollars. Johan took a deep breath and did not say anything. He was not sure what to say. Was he going to inherit all that wealth? What would he do with such an enormous amount of money?

"I will make it simple for you, Johan. Technically, all of this money belongs to your mom since she is officially still alive," explained Mr. Forrester.

The very mention of his mom brought back tears to Johan as he tried to hide his sorrow. Mr. Forrester paused for few seconds and continued.

"Your dad had asked us to put all this money into a trust which has been directed to pay out all of your college expenses. It will also pay you fifty thousand dollars a year for your other expenses. One more thing, the trust allows you to contribute up to one hundred thousand dollars a year to a charity of your choice."

Johan did not know what to say. Neither did he know what to do with all that money he was inheriting. But all that did not mater to him as the mention of his mother had completely clouded his thinking.

"Do you have any questions about the will, Johan?" Mr. Thompson tried to bring Johan back to the present as he seemed lost in his thoughts.

"No, I don't have any questions. I couldn't help thinking about my mom."

"Well, that brings us to the last thing we wanted to discuss with you. I don't want to get your hope too high, but, we just got a message from the PI team that they have some leads and think that your mom is alive," Mr. Forrester added as he handled all legal matters for Johan's dad.

When Johan heard that, there was a surge of excitement through his body. He felt dizzy and could not control his emotions. He was happy beyond his wildest imagination, and he wanted to know all the details. Mr. Forrester continued as he knew that Johan deserved more explanation.

"Well, as I said, I don't want to get your hopes too high. All they know is that some of their investigations have led them to believe that she is in India. As you know, India is a large country with more than a billion people. It may take forever to locate her even if the leads are true."

Johan did not pay much attention to what Mr. Forrester was saying. He did not want to want to rely on some private investigators to track down his mother. He knew it was his job; he was old enough to take that challenge. Moreover, there was enough money in the trust fund to help him with his mission and whatever else he wanted to do beyond that.

"I am going to India to track down my mom," Johan declared as Mr. Thompson and Mr. Forrester looked at him in bewilderment somewhat taken aback from the firmness in Johan's voice. They were still not convinced that going to India was the best route for their young friend. However, one look at his face convinced them that Johan was very serious about finding his mom, and they were ready to provide all the help he needed.

CHAPTER 14
Travel to India

Johan sat on the beige sofa in the living room staring at the wall not knowing where to begin his India journey. It was an old sofa his mom had bought from Foley's a long time ago. A lot had changed since that time; Foley's was now part of Macy's. From an outsider's perspective, nothing had changed - same stores, and same products. But Johan knew for the better; there were many lives that had been impacted by the change. He mused that his life was no different; so many things had changed in his life that he was arguably a different person inside, yet from an outside, for many, he was always the same Johan, one who was calm and collected.

He looked at the clock on the wall as it struck loudly announcing the arrival of the next day. A shadow entered the room as Kaya came to see how he was doing. Her left palm was closed as she sat next to him on the sofa and held his hand softly. Neither of them spoke a word until finally Johan spoke softly.

"I don't know where to start my India journey." Johan revealed his anxiety.

As a way of answering that question, Kaya brought her left fist forward and opened it to reveal a crumpled piece of paper as Johan carefully unfolded it to read what was written on it. There was just one word spelled in all capital letters which read "PRAYAG".

He looked at Kaya in puzzlement trying to understand what it meant as he had never heard that word before.

"I had a dream just now, and the yogi was in my dreams," she explained; she was obviously shaken a bit as it was something she had never expected.

"What did he say?" Johan almost jumped when Kaya mentioned the yogi.

"He said you should go to India and wait for him in Prayag. Someone will meet you there and take you to him."

"Prayag, I have never heard of this place. Did he tell you how to get there?"

"No, he did not tell me where it is; all he said was that one of his students would come and take you to him. He also said that you should be going there alone." Kaya was saddened as she explained the yogi's instructions.

"When I insisted that I should join you as well, he told me that there will be future occasions when I will have a chance to meet him." Johan could see that Kaya's eyes were watery as she realized that she would soon be separated from Johan for a long time.

Johan was also disappointed realizing that he could not take Kaya with him. Nevertheless, Johan felt energized so much so that he could feel his heart beating at its peak rate. He started perspiring heavily and felt like he was losing control of his senses – like a system that had experienced a sudden surge of energy.

They both logged onto their computers and searched the Internet to find that Prayag is a sacred place in North India at the confluence of the rivers Ganga and Yamuna.

"Maybe PK can help me get to Prayag. I am sure he can help." Johan spoke with a lot of enthusiasm while Kaya looked depressed.

"Let us get back to San Jose on the next available flight. I don't want to waste any time," declared Johan as he got up from the sofa. He had at last seen the light at the end of the dark tunnel that had oppressed his inner most emotions for the last few years.

His trip from Dallas to San Jose and the subsequent arrangements for the India trip had happened so fast that it all seemed surreal to him. PK had contacted his uncle in Delhi to meet Johan at the airport and take him to Prayag. Gopal Rao, PK's uncle, had assured them that he would help Johan find the Yogi.

Johan was a little nervous as he boarded the American Airlines flight from San Jose to Chicago. That was only the first leg of the journey as he had to change over to the Delhi flight at O'Hare. He knew that it was going to be a long journey, and India was a complete mystery to him. He had read many books on India; he had even watched some of the videos that were tailored towards American tourists. But he was not going there as a tourist, and he was least interested in visiting India's famous landmarks. His journey was a spiritual one which would take him to some unknown place in the Himalayas. But exactly where was that place? It was a complete mystery to him.

He decided to relax by listening to music reading a book as he eased into his seat. His seat was on the window side of first class, and an executive was sitting in the aisle seat next to him. As the plane took off and the flight attendant announced that they were free to use electronic devices, the man next to him took out his laptop and started working on a presentation. It looked like he was writing some sort of business proposal, and Johan did not bother to pay too much attention to him. Once the flight attendant served their drinks, he felt relaxed and started thinking about Mr. Gopal Rao, PK's uncle. PK had of course talked to his uncle to make sure that he would receive Johan at the Delhi airport. PK knew that without someone helping Johan, he would be lost at the airport. PK had always found the Delhi airport to be very confusing, almost like a jungle. He was genuinely concerned for Johan and wanted to make sure that Johan had a pleasant experience in Delhi and beyond. PK had made sure that Johan had stored Gopal Rao's phone number in his handset. Luckily, for Johan, his 3G phone worked all over the world including India.

"When you reach India, your phone will work. However, it is going to be very expensive to make calls using that phone," PK had advised.

"Yeah, I know. The stupid roaming charges will kick in. How much is it?" asked Johan.

"It can be two dollars a minute. My uncle has reserved a phone for you that you will be using in India," PK explained.

Johan was thankful for all the things PK had done for him. It was not as if he could not afford the expenses in India. He was now a very wealthy man beyond his imagination, but all of this wealth meant nothing to him. He was not going to buy a fancy car or a condominium in downtown San Francisco and change his life style overnight. In fact, he was not sure what he was going to do with that sudden wealth he had inherited. He often wondered if he could do something meaningful with that money to remember his dad and mom.

"I am truly grateful for all you have done, PK. I don't know how I am going to pay back." Johan remembered to thank his friend.

"No sweat, my friend. I want you to have a safe trip and a productive time in India. I was a little skeptical earlier whether you will be able to meet your yogi. The more I learn about your dreams and visions, the more I am inclined to believe that it will happen. You need to be very careful though."

PK was still worried that Johan was entering a dangerous zone and someone unscrupulous could exploit Johan's quest to meet the yogi.

"Don't worry about me, PK. I will be all right. Moreover, I have your uncle to help me," Johan smiled back.

All of his three friends had come to the airport to see him off; there was Nick and PK, and, of course, Kaya was there as well. All four of them had driven in Nick's car to the airport and had gone with him until the security gate. Nick was his usual self, lugging Johan's luggage and making jokes along the way while PK was a little anxious. He always got anxious whenever someone went on a long journey. The one who was worried the most was Kaya.

Few minutes before it was time for Johan to walk through the security gates, Kaya and Johan had walked away from their friends where they could have some private moments. Kay was in tears as she realized that Johan was going to be gone for a while tucked away somewhere in the Himalayas with no communication links whatsoever. It could be months or even years before she was going to see him again. This really broke her heart, and she started sobbing. Johan took her in his arms and tried to make her feel better knowing very well that whatever he would say was not going to stop her crying.

She did not say anything as she did not want to discuss anything anymore as she just wanted to embrace him as long a she could. When she finally did come out of the embrace, she said something that revealed her worst fears to Johan.

"What if something terrible happens to you, Johan? What am I going to do?" she asked Johan and started crying again.

"Nothing like that will happen to me, Kaya. I will be all right. I am going to find the Yogi and learn about all the mysteries behind my visions. I am also confident that he will help me find my mom. Don't worry. I will be back here in less than a year," Johan had assured her.

"Will you not forget me? Will you still love me?"

"Of course I will love you. There is nothing that will change that," Johan tried to assure her.

"You are sure?"

"Yes, I am one hundred percent sure. Will you wait for me until I come back?"

"Yes, I will Johan. I will wait for you forever," Kaya replied as she hugged him again. For some strange reason, Kaya felt like she had gone through the very conversation before like it was the second time Johan was going away from her which made her even more nervous. It was a feeling like from such a long time ago that it seemed like it was in one of her past lives. She wondered why she was getting that strange feeling within her but did not mention it to Johan.

Johan had to cut short his reminiscing as the flight attendant was making a loud announcement that the plane was about to land at O'Hare. Johan opened his eyes realizing that it was time for him to get ready to catch his flight to Delhi. As the plane touched the tarmac, the flight attendant was announcing that it was permissible for the passengers to turn their cell phones on. Johan pulled his phone from his pocket and promptly pressed the on button and within a second of turning his cell phone on, he heard a beep notifying him that there was a message waiting for him. He knew immediately it was from Kaya. She wanted to make sure that he had reached Chicago safely.

As the plane reached the gate, the passengers started getting up and crowding the passage between the seats as everyone wanted to be out as soon as possible. Johan took his backpack and started walking towards the exit. When he got out of the plane into the terminal and checked the gate information for his next flight, he saw that the Delhi flight was from Gate 18 on Concourse H. His plane had landed at Gate 20 on Concourse K. He looked at the map as he was not very familiar with the O'Hare airport, and realized that he had a considerable ground to cover. He did not mind the long walk as he had more than three hours left until the departure time for his Delhi flight.

As he started walking to his gate, he was amazed at the way the Concourse was brimming with people. It was like a busy mall full of passengers of all ages. It was the summer travel time, and he saw several families with kids. Of course, the kids were excited to be going on airplane. Johan carefully waded through the crowd and reached his gate area and sat down in a seat in a less crowded area and took his phone out. He read the message from Kaya. As he read the message, he could not suppress his emotions. He knew he was missing her and the thought of not being with her for the next several months was slowly sinking into his head. Suddenly, he felt lonely. He missed Nick and PK and their camaraderie. He pressed the button '2' which was the first button he could assign for speed calling. He heard Kaya's voice even before the phone rang. It was as if she was staring at her phone waiting for the call.

"Make sure you come back this time, Johan," Kaya blurted out subconsciously. She immediately knew that she did not make any sense. But she had no idea why those words came out of her mouth. However, Johan understood her mental state as he knew she was terribly depressed.

"If it makes you feel any better, I feel terribly lonely too," he replied.

"What can we do?" she asked almost reflexively.

"There is nothing we can do, Kaya. It is the karmic journey we need to endure, like PK says. This will only strengthen our love," he replied.

They finally ended the call when Johan heard the ground attendant making an announcement about boarding the plane.

Johan finally got onto the aircraft and sat in his business class seat, where he was quite comfortable. He was exhausted after that long conversation with Kaya and was eager to fall asleep. As he was settling down in his seat, an Indian business man came and sat next to him. After a brief chat, he introduced himself as Rajesh Balla and tried to strike a deeper conversation with Johan.

"Is this your first visit to India?" asked Rajesh.

"Yes, this is my first trip. I am just visiting my friend's relatives," replied Johan not eager to divulge the real purpose of his visit.

"Are you going to visit cities other than Delhi? You must see Jaipur and Udaipur. You should also see Agra," Rajesh advised Johan.

Johan knew that Taj Mahal was in Agra, and he also re-membered that there were some famous palaces and temples in Jaipur and Udaipur. He did not want to discourage Rajesh by telling him that he was not interested in any of them. His real interest was meeting the Yogi with the hope that he will help Johan find his mom. Again, Johan was not interested in revealing any of his plans. Moreover, his plans were murky and he was worried that anyone who heard his plans would think that he was strange or even worse deluded. Johan just nodded his head and smiled.

They were in the midst of this small talk for a while. Rajesh was a jewelry maker who came to US every three or four months to take orders for custom jewelry. He would bring designs from India and Italy and would market those designs to large jewelry chains. Once he got the orders, he would go back to India, get the jewelry made, and ship them to the chains, and he seemed to be happy with the way his business was doing. As they kept talking it was time for the plane to take off, and the flight attendant started making several announcements. Once they were in the air, things got quieter, and Rajesh started talking again. This time he started talking about diamonds.

"Do you know the most famous diamond is from India?" Rajesh began.

"You mean the Kohinoor diamond?"

"Yes, that is the one I am talking about, and that diamond is from India. The Queen should give it back to the temple in the South where it was originally found," Rajesh replied. He seemed a little agitated, and it was obvious to Johan that Rajesh had thought about the topic for a while.

"Seems like a fair deal to me. Why not? All colonial powers are trying to correct their wrongs and maybe someday, the Royal family will just do that," Johan suggested. "However, some in India think that it was a small price to pay for the service that the English did for India," Johan added. That statement surprised Rajesh.

"What type of service are you talking about?"

"Well, my friend PK says that without the English getting involved in the Indian geopolitics, India would have been run over by Islamic forces and would be an Islamic country by now," Johan explained.

Rajesh thought about that, and shook his head in disagreement.

"I do not agree with that statement. Islam had tried to convert India for more than a millennium and had failed. Look, it only took thirty years for Islam to run over Persia and wipe out the Zoroastrian faith there. They could never do that in India even after hundreds of invasions."

It was obvious that Rajesh knew his history and was a proud nationalist. Johan was, however, not in a mood to get into that debate, and he just nodded his head in agreement.

By that time, their dinner had arrived, and Johan chose the vegetarian plate. Once dinner was over, he fell asleep and did not know how long he had slept. What woke him up was the captain's announcement that they were just flying over Kabul, Afghanistan. Johan also noticed that the attendants were serving breakfast. He looked down through his window and could see the dusty buildings of Kabul. He saw a large mass of smoke, which told him that there were still some battles in progress in that area.

Before Johan got off from the plane, Rajesh gave his business card to Johan.

"You can always reach me if you need any help when you are in India. I have business associates all over the country, and we can help you with anything," Rajesh offered.

CHAPTER 15
In Search of Yogi

Johan and Gopal Rao reached Allahabad late in the evening and checked into a hotel named *Govinda Bhavan*. The hotel was not a luxury hotel, nothing close to the luxury hotel he had visited for lunch in Delhi just two days ago. It was more like a three star hotel, closer to the Fairfield Inn he used to frequent during his USTA tennis days in Texas. Johan did not mind that, and he reminded himself that his journey to India was a spiritual one and tried to stay focused. After they had checked into their rooms, Mr. Rao asked Johan to join him for dinner once he was refreshed which was perfectly all right with Johan as he was very hungry.

After they had refreshed in their rooms, they got together downstairs and walked to a restaurant not too far from the hotel. Johan could smell the aroma of curries, and it immediately reminded him of a restaurant he had visited in Dallas. He looked at the menu and noticed that it was vegetarian restaurant, and the menu claimed that they were an Udipi style restaurant. Johan had a flashback when he and Nick had once visited a restaurant called Udipi in Dallas. After Mr. Rao, finished ordering the food for both of them, Johan was curious about the name.

"What do they mean by Udipi style?" he asked Mr. Rao.

"Oh, Udipi is a holy place in the southern state of Karnataka. It has a famous temple of Lord Krishna," Mr. Rao explained. "People from Udipi are known for culinary talent, and they have started restaurants all over the world. You find them in New York to San Francisco in the US. In India you have Udipi restaurants in all cities and towns," Rao added.

Johan nodded his head. He was now getting used to spicy food, and his mouth was salivating with the spicy aroma that blanketed the entire dining area.

"What else is there in Udipi?" Johan replied as if to continue the conversation before the food arrived.

"I am awfully sorry, Johan. I should have first explained the significance of Udipi as a holy place. See, there is an amazing story behind the Lord Krishna temple. Some four hundred years ago, a warlord wanted to go inside the temple. However, the priests refused to let him in because they saw him as a 'low caste' person. Although such a grotesque practice is now illegal, such things may happen even these days in many rural areas, you know." Rao sounded very ashamed.

"Anyway, the warlord went behind the temple and sung a spontaneous melody that praised the Lord and at the same time begged the Lord to give him a view of His image and accept his prayers. An amazing thing happened; a sudden tremor caused an opening at the back of the temple where the warlord was standing, and the sculpture of Lord Krishna rotated so that His devotee could see Him." Rao was literally excited as he told that story to Johan. He then closed his eyes thinking about the temple which he had visited literally dozens of times.

"Who was that warlord? What else is known about him?" Johan asked obviously fascinated by the story.

"His name is Kanaka Dasa, and he went on to become a famous Hari Dasa, a servant of God, and to compose hundreds of hymns praising the Lord. His songs are choreographed to dance routines all over India even today," Mr. Rao explained.

Johan really liked that story and wanted to visit Udipi. Perhaps, the next time I am in India, he mused. His immediate goal was, of course, to meet the yogi.

"Are we going to start our search for the yogi right away?" asked Johan, obviously anxious to meet his guru.

"Let us just rest tonight, Johan. We can get up early in the morning and begin our search as soon as we are done with breakfast," advised Mr. Rao.

Johan was a little disappointed but did not mind retiring early that night as he was tired from the journey as well.

The next morning, Johan woke up before the dawn, took a long shower, and walked down to the breakfast area. He was there before Mr. Rao and patiently waited for his arrival. Within ten minutes, Rao joined him, and they both sat down for their breakfast.

"I suggest you have a heavy breakfast, Johan. I do not know how long we will be walking along the *Sangama* to find anyone who can help us," added Rao.

"Sangama? What do you mean by that?" asked Johan not following Rao.

"Sorry, Johan, I should explain. Sangama means confluence in Sanskrit. As I told you, Prayag is where the rivers Ganga and Yamuna merge into one which is a holy place for the followers of the Hindu faith. From what you told me, this is where Yogi's messenger is going to meet you," explained Rao.

As soon as they came out of the hotel, Amar, their driver, was waiting for them with the car ready. Soon, they were driving towards the sangama. When they reached a parking area, Amar parked the car, turned towards Rao, and explained in broken English.

"This is the closest we can come to the sangama. You will have to walk from here."

As soon as Johan and Rao got out of the car, a group of men surrounded them. They started talking to Rao in Hindi, and Rao was trying to get away from them and was replying in Hindi. Finally, when he succeeded in moving away from the crowd, Rao explained to Johan what was going on. They were all agents trying to take them to priests who would perform the right religious rites. Rao had told them that they were not there to perform any religious rites and were merely tourists who wanted to experience the sangama.

"I told them that the most we would do is take a dip in the sangama," said Rao.

As they both started walking along, there were literally hundreds of holy men dotting the banks of the river. They wore mostly in saffron robes and most of them were half-clad. They had various *mudras*⁹ on their forehead and body. Some were priests and some were mere sadhus (ascetics). None of them interested Mr. Rao, and he did not bother talking to any of them. They finally came near a large banyan tree near the river and decided to rest beneath the tree.

They rested under the tree for a while, when they saw a sadhu who was slowly approaching them. He looked very old and frail with long flowing hair, along with a long grey beard; several necklaces made up of different kinds of beads adored his neck. He had orange and yellow *mudras* on his chest and shoulders and he looked like he was more than one hundred years of age. He was so slender that there was

---

9   *Mudras are religious or spiritual symbols.*

absolutely no fat whatsoever on his body, and yet his posture was straight just like someone in his or her thirties. His eyes were sparkling, and there was no sign of tiredness or aloofness. Johan felt encouraged and hoped that he was the messenger who would take him to the yogi.

"Sadhu-ji, I am Gopal Rao, and this is Johan, my friend. He has come all the way from Texas seeking his guru. Perhaps, you can direct us to the yogi who can help Johan." Rao made the introduction while showing great respect for the old Sadhu.

The Sadhu smiled back with a twinkle in his eyes. "Texas, you mean America, right? Are you here seeking some sort of yogic power like many Americans who come here?"

"No, he is not seeking any power. He is here because he had a vision in which a yogi asked him to come here," explained Mr. Rao.

The whole conversation was in Hindi, and Johan had a real problem following. He however, was disappointed when he saw the old man shaking his head. He knew he was not the messenger.

"I am not the messenger. But I know the yogi you are talking about and he has mastered all dimensions of yogic power. Even other accomplished yogis consider him as a great one. Everyone calls him *Maha* Yogi[10]," replied the sadhu and started walking away from them. Suddenly he stopped and turned towards Mr. Rao and spoke slowly.

"Your messenger's name is Agni. He will be here soon," the old sadhu assured Mr. Rao.

"That is very kind of you, Sadhu-ji. When can we meet Agni?" asked Mr. Rao.

---

10 Maha *means great in Sanskrit.*

"Agni is never in one place. He travels along the holy Ganga. Sometimes he is here, sometimes he is in Varanasi or Haridwar, and many times he is where the holy Ganga meets the ocean," answered the Sadhu.

"So, you really do not know where he is right now?" Rao sounded disappointed.

"Do not worry about that. I will see if I can contact him," replied the old sadhu as he sat down and closed his eyes. He then went into a deep meditation. As he meditated, he stretched out his arms as if to reach something in the sky. Rao and Johan squatted few feet away from the sadhu and waited for him to open his eyes. The waiting seemed like hours although the sadhu was in that position for about ten minutes. He then opened his eyes and smiled at Johan.

"Good news for your friend; I sense that he will be here soon. I can just feel that. Stay in Prayag for few more days and keep coming here and you will meet him soon. You will know once you see him. No one can miss him," assured the sadhu.

"That is all I have for you. Now go back to your hotel. There is no need to waste your time here. The only one who can take you to Maha Yogi is Agni. You may want to take care of your business or do something that will keep you occupied," the sadhu encouraged them to leave the sangama area.

Johan and Rao really did not know what else to do either. They took that advice and went back to the hotel. For the next three days, they followed the same routine. They would finish their breakfast and come down to the sangama looking for Agni, but they had no luck in locating him. Surprisingly, they could not locate the sadhu either as he was nowhere in the area. Was the sadhu authentic? Rao and Johan had their moments of doubt. Nevertheless, something told them that they could trust the old Sadhu. Why would he want to lead astray a young disciple like Johan?

They kept wandering in the sangama area talking to other sadhus and holy men, and everyone they talked to assured them that they would eventually meet Agni. It was as if their story had traveled through the whole of Prayag like a wild fire. Nevertheless, all those assurances failed to reduce Johan's anxiety. Adding to Johan's anxiety was the fact that Gopal Rao was now getting a little worried and was thinking about his business back in Delhi. Rao wanted to help Johan as much as possible, but he had a business back in Delhi that needed his attention. He simply could not stay away from his affairs for a long time; he did carry out some of his business on his cell phone, but that was only a partial solution. He was ready to stay in Prayag for a maximum of two weeks. If they were unable to locate Agni Yogi in that period, he would have to leave Johan on his own.

Johan knew that his situation was getting untenable, and he could not expect Mr. Rao to help him indefinitely. He understood that Mr. Rao had a business to attend to and felt uncomfortable that they were on a wild goose chase looking for Agni. He took the first opportunity during dinner that night to encourage Rao to go back to Delhi.

"You know Mr. Rao, I am really grateful for all the things you have done for me. I am getting concerned that we do not seem to be going anywhere in finding Agni Yogi. If we do not find him in the next two days, you should go back to Delhi. I will somehow manage on my own," Johan brought up the subject knowing Rao was reluctant to broach the topic.

"That is all right, Johan. I can stay for a couple of weeks with you. I am sure we will find him in the next few days," Rao replied, trying to encourage Johan.

"I do not know how I can thank you Mr. Rao. I do not know why you are going to such a distance to help me." Johan was a little embarrassed as he felt that he did not deserve all that help.

"You know Johan, when I was a young man, I often fantasized about the special powers that come with yoga practice. I dreamt of becoming a yogi. The more I learn about your story, the more fascinated I am. This is the least I can do to help you," Rao replied.

The next morning they decided to spend more time at the river confluence, and decided to ask as many people as possible about Agni. They went about asking every other person about him.

"Have you seen Agni Yogi lately?" was their standard question. They did not know if he was old or young or how he looked. They had popped that question to so many people that every one knew who they were looking for, and many would answer them even before they asked the question. Of course, the answer was always negative.

It was almost evening, and the banks were getting less crowded. People who had come to the river to bathe or to do religious ceremonies had now left and the sangama was getting less crowded. As the dusk settled in, many sadhus and holy men had started fire for light and heat. Rao noticed that there was a man who was practicing yoga on a mat not too far from them and remembered that they had not seen him earlier. He turned to Johan and explained,

"Let us go and talk to that yogi. He will be the last one we will talk to today. If he cannot help us, let us come back tomorrow."

Johan agreed as he had no better idea. They walked to the yogi and waited for him to finish his routines. As they stood there waiting to speak to the man, they suddenly heard a voice from behind. As he heard that voice, Johan felt a surge of electricity through his body, and it was surreal not knowing exactly why he had such a feeling. Perhaps, it was because the strange voice was addressing him in English. Johan and Rao turned back to see who it was.

"So you are Johan, the young man looking for my master, and you are Gopal Rao helping him." The man who appeared to be a yogi addressed both of them.

Gopal Rao felt relieved to see the yogi. He was certain that it was Agni.

"Are you Agni Yogi?" he addressed the yogi who appeared to be very young. He was slim and tall with no fat whatsoever. He had long flowing hair along with a beard. Tanned and fit, his whole body appeared to be copper tone. He was also wearing beads and had several mudras on his chest and forehead. His body appeared to be glowing because of reflection from surrounding fires.

"Yes, I am Agni Yogi. You can call me just Agni. I am sorry I made you wait. I had to attend to a different task assigned to me by my master." Agni was very apologetic.

"That is all right. I am so happy to see you. I now know that all those visions I had over the years have a purpose and that the yogi is real," Johan replied trying hard to control his excitement.

"That is true, Johan. Our master is real although very few have met him in real life. Many young men from different parts of the world come here asking me to take them to my master. Very few have been able to keep up with the rigors of the journey. You know, he lives more than ten thousand feet in the Himalayas. Most of the seekers give up even before they reach my master. After they reach him, many cannot put up with his intense training regimen. So, Johan, tell me, are you up to the challenge?"

For some reason, it seemed that Agni did not know the whole story about Johan coming to Prayag. Johan was not in Prayag seeking any yogic power. He was there because the great yogi himself had summoned him to come there. His immediate goal was to find his mother, not to seek any power.

"I am ready for any hardship that comes along the way, Sir. I am dying to meet your master," Johan was determined as Rao watched them.

"It is good to see determination like that. Let us get together exactly at 6:00 AM at the same spot in two days. This will give you a day to prepare for the journey. Make sure that you have enough warm clothes. Remember we will be up in the mountains." Agni gave Johan specific instructions. "Any more questions before we part?" added Agni.

At that time, Johan started experiencing something strange. He felt like Agni was a large source of heat like a bonfire. It started feeling so hot around Agni that he felt like he was playing a tennis match in the hot West Texas sun, the times he had played a tournament in Abilene in August. He also noticed that Mr. Rao was not experiencing the same effect. He could not tolerate the heat anymore, and started perspiring profusely and started feeling dizzy. Gopal Rao who noticed this wondered what was wrong with Johan, and got a little worried. At that time, Agni put his hand over Johan's head and soon Johan started feeling normal.

"You will be all right, Johan. I think you will be a good student," assured Agni.

"What just happened here? Is everything all right?" asked concerned Rao obviously confused.

"There is nothing to worry, Gopal. When you have been a yogi for a long time like me, you give out yogic energy that only touches future yogis. This is one way I know those who want to meet my master have the true potential," explained Agni.

Gopal Rao understood at that point why everyone called him Agni Yogi. Agni in Sanskrit means fire, and it was obvious that other yogis sensed that. Rao was intrigued that Agni had referred to himself as an old yogi although he barely looked thirty years old.

"May I ask you how long you have been a yogi, Agni?" asked Rao.

"Not very long; I have been a student of Maha Yogi for around a hundred years," he calmly replied.

Gopal Rao found it hard to believe, but he was not very surprised. He had read about the power of yoga on human health, both physical and spiritual. Never had he imagined that someone could be more than one hundred years old and look less than forty years of age. He only wished that he could walk away from his business and just join Johan and Agni on that mysterious quest. He knew it was only a momentary wish; the power of material world was too much for him to overcome.

The next day, Rao and Johan were busy shopping. Rao made sure that Johan had lots of dry fruits, Ayurvedic energy tablets and medicine, some extra sweaters and jackets. Johan's backpack was now overflowing with clothes and other essentials. He felt good that he had brought one of those large brand name hiking backpack. Rao also bought him a GPS device in case Johan lost his direction in the mountains.

The next day came fast and both were up very early in the morning. Rao had requested a special delivery of breakfast for them, which they finished before five in the morning. Soon they were at the same spot where they had met Agni just two days ago. Johan looked at his watch and noticed that there was at least ten more minutes to six AM. He was confident that Agni was joining them in few minutes and felt relaxed. His bags were still in the car that was a few miles away as he did not know exactly what his yogi guide had in mind.

"I see Agni coming our way. He seems to have few more holy men with him," Rao noticed a group of men walking in their direction almost five hundred yards away. Johan turned in that direction and nodded his head a little puzzled about the other holy men.

"You are all prepared Johan? Have you thought about it some more and have no qualms about coming with me to the mountains?" Agni asked as he and his friends joined Johan and Rao.

"I am absolutely certain about that Agni. No qualms whatsoever," replied Johan having real difficulty withholding his excitement.

"That is good, Johan. These five are my friends who want to travel with us in the train until Kanpur. From there they will continue to Delhi, whereas we will take a bus and travel north to the bottom of the Himalayas," Agni explained. "We will reach a small town called *Kashi Pura* at the bottom of the mountains by around 10 PM. We will sleep there in the local temple, and start our journey up the mountains. My Guru lives in the mountains between *Badrinath*[11] and *Nanda Devi*[12]," added Agni. He then turned to Rao to instruct his part.

---

11 *A holy place in the Himalayas that is famous for the Lord Badrinath Temple. It is more than ten thousand feet above the sea level.*

12 *One of the highest peaks (25, 345 feet) in the Himalayan range.*

"Gopal, I will come with you and Johan in the car. Take us to the railway station, and my friends will join us soon."

Agni's friends soon parted and were on their way to the railway station, while Johan and Gopal Rao along with Agni walked to the car. When Amar had driven them all to the station, Gopal Rao went and bought tickets for Johan and Agni as well as tickets for Agni's friends. Within a few minutes, the other five yogis joined them emerging from the shadows as if they were already there. The five yogis had reached the station so fast that Johan wondered if they had flown from Sangama to the station. Johan even wondered if he was witnessing a glimpse of their yogic power.

As they all walked into the railway station, and got ready to board the train that was already on the platform, Gopal Rao got somewhat emotional. He hugged Johan, wished him good luck, and stood there as all the six yogis and Johan got into the train. Soon the train was on its way to Kanpur, and Johan wondered when he was going to see Gopal Rao again as he waved at him while the train slowly moved away from the platform.

The six yogis sat together in the rail car while Johan sat alone on a side chair. He noticed that the yogis hardly talked, and soon they all went into deep meditation. Johan tried to meditate as well; he could not really concentrate as all the noise from the surrounding passengers kept disturbing his focus. He wondered how those six yogis could get into such a deep meditative state so easily. The train kept accelerating, and it was now moving fast. Johan kept staring at the outside scenery, which was a mixture of green and brown landscape with occasional farm animals dotting the fields.

Within a few hours, they had reached the Kanpur station, which was extremely busy and crowded. There was hardly any place for people to get down from the train and move around. Even in that seemingly chaotic situation, people got on with their businesses. There were families getting down their luggage with the help of porters, and at the same time other families getting into the train cars, and in the middle of all this, several vendors were moving from car to car, selling fruits, tea, and snacks. Johan and Agni got down from the rail car as Agni bid goodbye to his friends. Johan had his heavy backpack while Agni had a small bag tied to his waist and another bag that he carried in his hand. They managed to get out of the station and started walking towards the bus station. When they came to the bus station, Johan noticed that there were dozens of red and blue busses with agents trying to steer people to their respective buses. Agni knew exactly which bus to take as they walked into a red bus that said "Kashi Pura". As they got into the bus, Johan took out some rupees from his wallet and bought tickets for both of them. Soon they were traveling north of Kanpur towards Kashi Pura. The bus was very old and the engine seemed overworked. As they traveled north along a state highway, Johan looked around, amazed at the way the conductor had packed the bus with people; the bus was literally overflowing with people. There were around fifty people seated while another twenty people stood between the seats and held on to the rail attached to the bus's ceiling. Many of them swayed from side to side as the bus tried to avoid a series of potholes on the highway.

Johan was getting hungry and he decided to take out some food that Gopal Rao had bought for him and started eating it slowly. Agni, who was next to him, noticed it and shook his head in disagreement.

"The food you are eating is poison. It will destroy your body over the years," he declared, disapproving of Johan's food. Johan was a little puzzled as he was eating some bread and fruits. He did not know why Agni felt that way. Agni took out a jar from his bag that had some sort of paste that looked almost like dark peanut butter.

"I want you to eat this. One spoon of this will give you all the energy you need for the whole day. I have few bottles in the bag that should last us for several weeks," he explained as he put a spoon of that paste into Johan's palm.

Johan stared at the paste for few seconds and hesitated not knowing how it was going to taste. In the end he decided to eat it; after all, he wanted to be a yogi and the best way to begin the transformation was to become acclimated to the food habits of yogis. To his surprise, he found the taste to be delightful and was tempted to ask for some more of the paste.

"I know it is tempting to eat more. All you really need is one spoon per day. That and pure water whenever you get thirsty is all you need," explained Agni smiling.

Within minutes, Johan started feeling energized so much that he wanted to go on a tennis court and play a five set match. He had never felt that energized in his life and felt as if he was ready for anything, even to move a mountain.

It was six hours since they had left Kanpur. The driver had made several stops along the way, mostly at small towns and villages. They were now entering a region that was beginning to look like the beginning of the Himalayan range. They could even see the taller mountains a few miles away. The vegetation was getting thicker and greener. Suddenly, in the middle of nowhere, Agni got up and started pulling the bell indicating that he wanted to get down. The driver stopped while at the same time explained to Agni that he would not normally do this for anyone, but he was doing this because Agni was a yogi. Agni smiled back and thanked him as he and Johan got out of the bus. As they started walking away from the bus along a trail that branched off from the high way, Agni asked Johan to stop and put his hand on his head. Right at that moment, Johan felt like a high voltage surge was going through his body. It happened so fast that he felt like he rocketed out of earth to an altogether a different realm. He was scared like never before and felt dizzy and closed his eyes for a few moments. When he opened his eyes, everything surrounding him seemed surreal. He was still on planet Earth all right; however, it seemed that everything around him was in slow motion. Everything except for Agni was in slow motion. While he and Agni were walking at a normal pace, the birds in the sky were moving so slowly that it was like watching a movie on the National Geographic channel. He then looked at the bus, which looked like it was hardly crawling. Johan noticed that the trail they were on was turning back towards the highway a few miles from where they had dismounted the bus. He also noticed that the both the highway and the trail had a steep curve where they came together. On the other side of the winding road was a vertical fall of more than two hundred feet. Johan's heart started beating incredibly fast as he realized that he was going to experience his first yogic moment.

They both reached the point where the road and the trail merged and waited for the bus to arrive. As the bus turned to stay on the road, it skidded and started going down the cliff. Right then, Agni took a deep breath, sat on his knees, and pushed the bus back to the road towards the center of the road so that it could continue with its journey. Johan was flabbergasted with what he had just witnessed and was shaking with excitement. He did not know what to say and just stood there, eyes widened and mouth open. Agni put his hand back on Johan's head to calm him down which brought him back to the normal realm. Everything was moving normally now; things looked so normal that it was as if none of the things he had witnessed had ever happened. The driver of the bus noticed the two of them and stopped the bus for them.

As he opened the door to let them back in, he exclaimed, "Yogi Brother, why can't you make up your mind? You want to walk or you want to ride the bus?"

The driver then looked at one of the passengers and explained, "This is not the first time he has done that."

As he took his seat, Johan wondered how Agni could do what he had just witnessed. He realized that with his yogic power, Agni was able to propel into a different realm where time traveled thousands of times faster than it did on Earth. That gave him the speed advantage to make adjustments. At least that was the explanation he could come up with. However, how did he know there was going to be an accident? There was so much for him to learn that he felt humbled.

CHAPTER 16
Reaching the Maha Yogi

Johan and Agni got out of the bus as soon as they reached Kashi Pura and walked towards a temple that was not too far from the bus station. Several people had already gathered inside the temple as it was time for the evening *Arati*.[13]

Johan noticed that it was a Shiva temple. They kept their footwear outside the entrance to the temple and entered the compound, the bells started ringing, and the worshippers started singing a song praising Lord Shiva. After the arati was over, the priest distributed Prasada to devotees. Both Agni and Johan ate the Prasada and sat inside the temple hall. Slowly, the crowd started dispersing from the temple and the hall became empty except for some older people and the priests who were engaged in some local discussions. Meanwhile, Agni was into deep meditation, and Johan did his best to meditate as well. As he was yet to master the technique of meditation, he had a little trouble entering the deep meditative state. It was now 9 PM, and it was time to close the temple door and the gate. The priest walked to Agni and enquired if they were going to stay overnight in

---

13 *Worship service.*

the temple. When Agni nodded his head affirmatively, he went inside and brought a couple of pillows, blankets, and mats.

"Agni, you and your friend can sleep on that covered platform. You know the routine. If you leave before I come in the morning, just leave these in the corner," the priest explained as he handed over the blankets and mats to them. He later locked the door to the temple, went outside the compound, and locked the gate as he went home.

"How are we going to get out of the temple if we wanted to leave early in the morning?" Johan was a little concerned. Of course, he did not want to lose even a minute in reaching the Maha Yogi.

"Do not worry, Johan. Just leave that to me. What I want you to do is to start honing your meditation skills tonight," assured Agni.

"How do I do that?" Johan did not attempt to hide his frustration.

"Start concentrating on the Divine. God's presence is everywhere including your own heart, and the best way to focus is to look into your own heart. I will teach you a mantra. Repeat it in your mind as you focus on the Divine. Repeat the mantra *Om Namo Narayana* as you exhale," explained Agni.

Johan knew the word Om as the symbol for God. However, he did not know the meaning of the word *Narayana*, although he remembered that the yogi himself had taught him that mantra in one of his dreams. Seeing his puzzled look, Agni explained, "Narayana is one of the Sanskrit names for God Almighty. It literally means abode for all humans. Of course, the ultimate abode for all of us is God."

As Johan tried to hone his meditation skills using the sacred mantra, he was amazed how easily his mind was able to discard all the extraneous thoughts that always cluttered his mind during meditation. Soon he was in a deep meditative state; this was a first time experience for him. He felt light and free, so light and free that he felt that he was floating above the towering Himalayan peaks. When he finally completed his mediation and opened his eyes, he saw that Agni was still in his trance and decided to fall asleep. He felt cleansed deep inside and was in such a relaxed state that he was deep asleep in a matter of seconds.

"Get up, Johan; it is time for our next phase of the journey. One more day, and you will be ready for the final leg of your journey," Agni tried to wake up his newfound companion. Johan opened his eyes and saw that it was still dark.

"What time is it? It is still dark everywhere," Johan sounded a little concerned.

"We will hike up the mountains for about two hours. We will reach a hot spring where we are going to take a dip in hot water that will cleanse your body and mind. After that, we will hike for another eight hours. We will come to a place called *Devi Ghat*. I will explain the significance of that place when we reach there. Of course, we will rest along the way," explained Agni.

Johan got up very excited hearing that in just forty-eight hours he was going to see his long sought-after guru. The way Agni explained it, there was bound to be some more excitement along the way. They both rolled the blankets and mats and placed them in the storage area and were ready to leave the compound. At that instant, Johan remembered that the priest had locked the gates the previous night, and the temple compound wall was more than ten feet tall. He wondered how Agni was going to get them out of the temple. Perhaps, he is going to use his mental powers to unlock the gates, he reasoned. Johan felt goose bumps just thinking about that possibility.

To his astonishment, nothing of that sort happened and what ensued next was even beyond his imagination. His jaws dropped as Agni started lifting himself into the sky, and floated across the compound wall and landed outside on the other side the wall as Johan exclaimed in his own mind. *I cannot believe it! Agni is a flying Yogi!* Johan rubbed his eyes and pinched his arms to make sure that it was not a dream. He then heard Agni giving him specific instructions to get ready for a big surprise.

"Stay still, Johan. I will take you to the other side," which startled Johan as he felt that the voice was just one foot away from him. Before he could even reason what was going on, he felt like he was hit by a surge of electricity that made him lose his footing and for a moment he felt unconscious. As he regained his balance, he felt that another person had entered his body, and he felt petrified and froze. *What is it happening to me? Is Agni inside me now?* Then he heard Agni's voice in his head like it was coming from his own mind.

"Do not worry about me, Johan. I will be inside you for just few more seconds. I will take you over the wall, and once we are outside, you will be back to normal."

Before Johan could even reply, he could sense that his body started floating upwards like some unseen force was gently lifting him off the ground. He slowly floated across the wall and landed softly on the other side where he saw Agni's body laying flat on the ground. All this took less than fifteen seconds, and Johan was dumbfounded and did not know what to say. Just when he was about to accept Agni as a resident of his body, he felt another violent gyration inside his body and fell down as he lost his balance again. He lifted his head to see what was going on, and realized that Agni had left his body and had gone back to his own body as they both got back on their feet.

"I am sorry if the whole experience startled you, Johan. That was the easiest way for us to leave the temple without waiting for the priest to return," Agni explained almost apologetically.

"That was all right. What happened here? Can you explain this yogic power to me?"

"Yes, what you experienced is one of the highest yogic powers called Para Kaya Pravesha, or parallel body experience. I thought that you should experience this yogic power as you would need that power sometime in the future. This is a power you will be able to master once you have been initiated by my guru," Agni added which sent waves of excitement through Johan's mind. So Agni knows about my mission; he was merely testing me earlier, he mused.

"Thanks for that experience. I liked it very much, Agni. It was fascinating and I just cannot wait to learn that power now that I have witnessed it myself."

"Did you ever think that such a thing can really be done?"

"I had read powers such as these in stories but never really thought that it could be done."

Johan still wondered how that power was going to help him find his mom.

Johan and Agni quickly left Kashi Pura and were soon on the trail that went to Badrinath more than ten thousand feet above sea level. As it was still dark, they could see the stars and the crescent moon which gave them enough light to stay their course on the trail. They had traveled for about two hours when sun started coming up and the majesty of the Himalayas became obvious to Johan. The air was cool and dry, and the morning sunrays added a bit of warmth to the surroundings. The snow covered mountain peaks seemed like distant temple steeples similar to the one he had seen in Kashi Pura.

They finally reached an area of the trail where there were groups of large rocks on one side that caught Johan's attention. He marveled at the majesty of those rocks and estimated that some of the rocks were as tall as sixty to eighty feet. While Johan was fascinated by the scenery, Agni stopped near the rocks, looked at his young companion, and explained his next step.

"This trail keeps going to Badrinath, but we are going to deviate from the trail and go in the western direction," he explained, pointing towards the rocks. Johan looked towards the rocks to see if there was any trail for them to follow. There was no such thing and all he could see were those monstrous rocks and the dense forest behind the rocks.

"I do not see any trail in that direction. How are we going to climb those rocks?" Johan asked. This time he was less anxious; in the worst case, Agni could help him fly above the rocks.

"Let us just go around the first two rocks," whispered Agni, not giving him any hint of what was ahead.

When they went behind the second rock, Johan noticed that the second and third rocks were very close to each other and there was hardly enough space for them to walk freely. As they carefully managed to get between the two rocks, Agni signaled Johan to stay there, and went ahead and pressed a smaller rock that was few feet from Johan. Something unexpected happened at that moment and a large chunk of the third rock rotated, opening a passageway that went down several feet.

As Johan and Agni entered the passage, a small oil lamp was shimmering inside a hole in the wall. Agni took a torch that was next to the lamp and lit, allowing them to see the steps that went down several feet. Johan noticed that there was an Om[14] written on one of the rocks sitting on the edge of the wall. Agni went and pressed his right hand against the Om, and a creaking noise came out and the rock at the entrance went back to its original position closing the opening to the passageway.

After they had traveled around fifty feet downwards, the passageway stopped going down and it now became a flat tunnel, just tall enough for Johan and Agni to walk freely. They traveled along that tunnel for almost two miles when they came to the end. Johan noticed that similar to the place where they had entered the passageway, there was a small rock on the wall with the symbol Om carved on it along with a shimmering lamp near by. Agni asked Johan to put his right hand on Om and press it hard. Johan was more than eager to follow the instructions and the rock at the end of the tunnel made a loud noise as it slowly turned outward, creating an opening for them to leave the tunnel. At that point, Agni turned off the torch and placed it on a hook attached to the wall, and they both came out of the tunnel. Agni promptly walked towards a small rock that was just outside the tunnel and turned the rock to close the entrance to the tunnel.

Johan and Agni both stood just outside the tunnel for a minute admiring the picturesque Himalayan scenery that was in front of them. Johan observed that what was ahead of them was really a dense subtropical forest full of tall lush trees.

"Let us trek up this range for about two hours. We will come to a hot spring area where we can take a relaxing dip,"

---

14 *Om is a scared symbol denoting God. Bhagavad Gita 9.17:* I am the sacred symbol Om.

Agni explained. That was perfectly all right with Johan as he was a little tired and wanted to relax.

As they walked up the mountain, the forest area began to get denser, so dense that Johan could hardly see any sunrays reaching the floor of the forest. He started hearing strange sounds of Himalayan wild; sounds he had never heard before that seemed eerie and made him feel anxious. *What if some wild animal attacks us? How are we going to defend ourselves?* These were just a few of the questions swirling inside his head. As if he had read Johan's mind, Agni tried to reassure him.

"The wild animals are not going to attack us, Johan. As long as we do not harm them, they will leave us alone. Trust me on this."

Of course, Johan trusted Agni, but it was only his nature to worry about such things. Finally, they came to an area where the mountain had reached a plateau. Johan noticed that there was a spring that drained into a pond and the steam emanating from the gushing spring made it clear that the water was very hot. Nevertheless, Johan was excited to see that pristine hot water pond and was eager to take a relaxing dip. They both slowly waded into the pond until the water level came up to their chest level. Johan had never felt so relaxed in his life as he slowly swam across to the end of the pond and submerged his entire body except for his face inside hot water. He then took some water in his palms and washed his face. As he looked at the tall mountain peaks surrounding the plateau, he was awestruck by the breathtaking beauty of the surrounding mountain ranges. Soon, Agni swam towards Johan and sat not too far from him. They did not say anything to one another and it was as if neither of them wanted any interference as they absorbed the serenity emanating from the wild. Soon, both of them closed their eyes and started to meditate.

When Johan opened his eyes, he had the biggest scare of his life. Not too far from him on the edge of the pond was a large wild tiger stretching his front legs. His posture looked like he was getting ready to pounce on Johan and Agni which gave Johan a chill through his spine, and he could hardly speak. He looked at Agni who was staring at the tiger as if the tiger and he were communicating to one another. The tiger slowly got up, walked around the pond, and came close to Agni as he leaned on his side and licked Agni's face, which astonished Johan. A wild tiger behaving like a house cat. How could that be possible? However, as he spent more time with Agni, nothing really surprised Johan anymore. He was beginning to understand the yogic power. He remembered that he had read in books that yogis had the power to read minds including that of animals, and were able to communicate silently.

"Raja, this is Johan, my friend. Say hello to him," Agni prompted the tiger.

The tiger came towards Johan and licked his face, causing Johan to freeze with uncontrollable fear.

"There is nothing to be afraid of, Johan. Raja is a good friend. He will help you anytime you are in trouble," assured Agni.

The tiger walked away from Johan, bowed to both of them, and quickly ran back into the woods.

"See, Johan, the tiger is the most graceful animal in the wild. A hundred years ago, there were more than forty thousand tigers in India, and today, we have less than two thousand of them. It is all because of hunting and poaching." Agni sounded extremely sad.

Johan could feel Agni's anguish. It was obvious that for Agni, tiger was more than just a wild animal as he had a spiritual connection to the big cat.

"Today's problem is no more hunting as hunting of tigers is illegal. The real culprit is poaching that caters to a growing demand in countries like China and Taiwan," he continued.

"What sort of demand?" Johan was a little puzzled.

"In those countries they believe that parts of a tiger can cure many ailments; it is all nonsense. Nevertheless, they are ready to pay top dollars. When there is a market, there is always someone ready to do the dirty work," explained Agni.

Johan did not say anything as he did not know what to say that would make Agni feel better. He kept thinking that there must be a solution, and the long silence continued.

Finally, when they felt refreshed enough to continue with their journey.

"By early evening we should be near Devi Ghat. At that time, I will have to part with you. The last leg of the journey to my guru is about a two thousand feet climb. Any one who wants to reach him has to do it alone," explained Agni.

Although that worried Johan a little bit, he was ready for the challenge, and at the same time, he was a little sad that Agni was going to be gone soon. He was beginning to feel like he was an old friend, the way he felt towards Nick back home.

It was early evening when they reached another plateau area. What caught Johan's attention was a large rock nearby that had an image of Goddess Durga sketched on it. The artist had painted the sketch that made Her look almost life like. Agni stopped and pointed at the image.

"Look how beautiful She looks. That is Goddess Durga. She personifies the Divine energy found in the material world." Agni was full of reverence as they both approached the carving. "I will tell you a story behind Her power, Johan. People worship Her for saving the human race from a menacing buffalo headed demon. This buffalo headed demon had a boon that no male could kill him. Goddess Durga, riding a Tiger, came down to earth to destroy the evil buffalo headed demon," Agni explained the significance of Durga worship.

"It is too sad that the tiger, which is an integral part of the Goddess religion, is on the verge of extinction. The only thing we can do is to pray to Her to save the tigers," he repeated his concern for the wild cat's survival. He then turned right and pointed towards some stone steps.

"These steps go down towards Devi Ghat. There is a natural pond there. I am going to go there for a drink," Agni stated. It was as though he was bidding goodbye to Johan.

"The water in Devi Ghat removes any ailments you may have. Indeed, it has an anti-aging power. However, for the water to be effective, you have to be a real yogi," Agni explained.

Johan nodded his head as he quickly sensed that Agni was going to leave him soon. He waited for Agni's next instruction and hoped that he would give him some advice about the last part of his journey. Agni pointed west towards the large rocks that looked like they were stacked on one another.

"Do you see those large rocks there, Johan? They are the four rocks that you need to climb; each rock is about five hundred feet tall. When you reach the top, you will see my guru," explained Agni with a sense of relief that he had done his part. After all, his job was to bring most promising young men and women to his guru to keep the yogic tradition alive. He was like a recruiter for the Maha Yogi.

He also knew that in Johan's case it went beyond recruiting a promising student. He knew Johan was there on a special mission that went beyond finding his mom.

When Johan looked at the rocks, he was almost disheartened. The rocks were huge and each of them had a vertical climb and the task that was ahead of him seemed like climbing El Capitan four times in succession. Johan had never done any rock climbing nor was he equipped with the gear that is required for such an adventure. But Agni read what was going on in his mind and gave Johan his advice.

"Yes, it is a very difficult task, Johan. However, it is not impossible. You do not need any rock climbing gear either. You cannot see from here, but when you go near the rocks, you will see two ropes coming down from the top. One is real and the other is an illusion. Hold on to the one that is real and just keep climbing; the only way you can reach the top is if you grab the real one first," Agni explained.

"How would I know which one is real and which one is an illusion?"

"It all comes down to focus. It all comes down to getting rid of the clutter that clouds your mind."

Johan turned towards the rocks and kept thinking about the challenge that seemed almost insurmountable from his vantage point. Agni's advice kept echoing in his mind. *It all comes down to focus; I can do it,* he encouraged himself. He then turned towards Agni to thank him, but to his dismay, Agni was nowhere in the vicinity as if he had vanished into thin air. Johan was very upset that he had not even thanked him. He kept searching for Agni for a while, but he knew quite well that it was futile given the yogic powers that Agni possessed.

Johan walked towards a nearby rock and sat on it to get his thoughts together. He had to tread very carefully from this point on knowing that there was no one to hold his hand if he ever made a misstep. Johan did not know how long he stayed there until he realized that he had to continue with his journey. Any more delay would only complicate his climb as the sun was going to set within the next few hours.

Johan got up and started walking towards the rocks, and as he came near the bottom of the first rock, he gazed up to look for the ropes. Agni was right, there were two strong ropes coming down from the top. He remembered Agni's advice and tried to focus as hard as he could to find the real rope. It did not help him as he was still unable to distinguish between the two, and he still did not know which one was real and which one was an illusion. He decided to close his eyes and meditate, and when he came out of his meditation and looked at the ropes again, he noticed that the rope to the left looked crumpled like it was made of ash. Johan knew immediately which one was real, and he grabbed the right one and started climbing one-step at a time ever so carefully. He was amazed at the ease with which he could move forward as he kept his focus in place. When he reached the top of the first rock, he stood there for a minute just to look at the nature surrounding him and to garner some strength. He was soon focusing on the task of climbing; this time as he focused on the ropes, he realized that the real rope was the left one and in less than an hour, he was at the top of the second rock. He was now half way to the guru he was seeking. Next in line was the third rock, which looked steeper than the first two. Johan knew he had to focus harder this time and he decided to meditate some more. When he opened his eyes, there it was right in front of him; the real rope on the right side and the illusionary one on the left side. The rest of his climb was easy although the rock was the steepest so far. When he reached the top of the third rock, he was ecstatic. All that was remaining was one more rock to climb. He felt like a veteran now, and he felt proud of his accomplishment. He knew the routine now - right, left, and right. He grabbed the rope to the left and started climbing and he kept moving fast as he could; he was anxious to reach the top as soon as possible.

He had moved up by about one hundred feet when something unthinkable happened. It started getting dark and the rope he was holding started crumbling as if it had caught a fire and soon it was a rope of ashes. Johan lost his grip and started falling down. He let out a loud scream that echoed through the mountain ranges as he fell down with his head down. He knew he had committed a mortal mistake; he had gotten overconfident and had neglected to focus. *Oh, guru, please forgive me,* he cried in his mind and then suddenly as if the great yogi heard his cry, a strong wind started lifting him. The force of the wind was so much that he felt pushed upwards. In fact, he was slowly moving upwards like a hot air balloon. He felt as if he was a toddler again with his mother holding his hand and helping him as he tried to walk. Soon he had reached the top, and to his amazement, he was standing right in front of Maha Yogi, who seemed to be in deep meditation. It had all happened so fast that Johan felt utterly disoriented, and it took him several minutes to regain his bearing.

CHAPTER 17
The Training

Johan stood for almost ten minutes not knowing how exactly he had reached the top. The thrill of finally reaching his long cherished goal and seeing his spiritual master was so overwhelming that he had tears in his eyes. Overcome by a surge of emotions, he sat down to control his feelings. That was to no avail as his whole body kept shaking, and he was experiencing emotions that were altogether foreign to him. After a long while, once he took control of his senses, he felt relaxed and serene that he had finally accomplished his goal. He took his backpack, placed it on the ground, and stretched his hands upwards and quietly gave out a joyous cry of accomplishment. He was surprised at his outburst, and he knew that it was the outcome of accomplishing something that for a long time had seemed unreachable; he finally felt like a free man. He then looked around the area to get a sense of the surroundings. He was amazed that he was on an extremely flat area at the top of the mountain. On one side was a large cave, and at the other end was a large tree. Below the tree was an area that almost looked like a stone platform. There he was, the Maha Yogi seated in the lotus position doing his meditation. Johan had an instant feeling of reverence towards the great yogi. He had finally met his guru, the guru who had communicated with him since the days of his childhood. Now that he had come face to face with his master, he had never felt so poignant in his entire life.

Johan stood there silently waiting for the yogi to come out of his meditation. Not knowing what to do next, he decided to sit on a rock nearby. He did not know how long he had to wait there. What worried him were the stories he had read where yogis often meditated for weeks and he prayed that the great yogi would come of out of his meditation soon.

Johan wondered how the Maha Yogi would help him find his mother. Would he teach him some of the yogic powers he had experienced first hand from Agni during his journey to the master? Did his master have any more tasks beyond finding his mother on his mind? While waiting for his guru, he remembered a story he had read about a Zen master. It was about a young man who goes to the master to find the answer to the meaning of life. In that story, the young seeker, just like Johan, climbed a mountain and waited for the Zen master to come out of his meditation. When he finally came out of the meditative state, the young man asked his question, the master just stared at the young seeker and splashed a cup of tea on the young seeker's face. Disappointed, the young man goes home and comes back the next day to witness the same outcome. This happens three times when it finally dawns on the young seeker that the meaning of life was for him to find out and not for the master to explain. Such was the wisdom of the Zen master.

As Johan thought about that story, he wondered if the great yogi would do something like that. He felt ridiculous thinking about it. Wasn't it the yogi himself who had sent him the specific message asking him to come to Prayag?

Wasn't he the one who had sent Agni to bring him here? He knew he was being ridiculous. Just then, out of nowhere, he heard the familiar voice that was unmistakably the voice of Agni.

"He will not do anything of that sort, Johan."

Johan got excited. He was not surprised to hear Agni's voice as he knew that yogis had the power to materialize and dematerialize as they wished.

"Where are you, Agni? Can I see you?"

At that point, Agni appeared right in front of him just a few feet away from him. He stood there with a big smile on his face.

"I am so happy to see you, Agni. I felt terrible that I had not even thanked you for all the help you have given me," Johan said in an excited voice.

"That is nothing, Johan. The important thing is you have safely reached the top," Agni replied.

"Well, I almost did not make it. When I was climbing the fourth rock, I slipped and fell down. I do not know how I came here, but somehow I floated to the top," Johan explained.

"I know that. Who do you think brought you here? It was not easy, you know. You are not a small man to push upwards," laughed Agni as he explained how he had stopped Johan from falling.

"It was you, Agni? I do not know how I can repay you," replied Johan, sounding even more grateful.

"You will have plenty of opportunities to help others. Thinking about the present, my guru will not come out of his meditation until the morning. I suggest that you take some rest tonight. That way, when you meet the master, you will be full of energy. You may want to sleep inside the cave."

Johan nodded his head as it seemed like a good suggestion.

"Johan, this time around, I am really going to leave you. I will go back to Prayag. I am confident that you will do well under the master, and you will accomplish your goal," Agni explained.

Johan got emotional as he instantly embraced Agni, and within a few moments, he realized that he was embracing thin air as Agni had disappeared.

Johan slowly walked towards his bag, picked it up, and entered the cave. The cave was large with a shimmering lamp at the far end to keep it lighted. Johan was so exhausted from his long journey and all the unexpected twists and turns he had experienced along the trek that he was deep asleep the moment he had lain down on the floor of the cave.

Deep in his sleep, he heard the yogi calling him, the same way he had heard him for the first time in Plano, Texas. He quickly got up and went towards the yogi, and he was somewhat disappointed to see him still meditating.

"I am so happy you are finally here, Johan. How are you feeling?" He heard the yogi's voice inside his head. He was still communicating with Johan by telepathy.

How does he do it? Wondered Johan as he tried to answer him.

"I know you have gone through a lot of emotional turmoil in your young life. I will help you find your mom. Before I can help you with that, you need to become a real yogi. You need to acquire many yogic powers. Yogic powers such as telepathy and levitation. You will have to learn trans-migration of souls. These powers will not only help you find your mom, but you will also need them for another important mission I have in mind for you. Are you ready for all of this, Johan?"

Johan was ready to do anything his master wanted him to do. The yogi, of course, knew it.

Before he could answer the question, he felt warm sun-rays hitting his face which woke him up from his dream.

Johan sat down, stretched his arms, and looked around to make sure that he was still not in a dream. He wanted to make sure that he had really reached the yogi and that it was not one of his wild dreams. He looked around to see any sign of the yogi. Finally, he walked out of the cave and looked towards the tree to see if the yogi was still beneath the tree. To his surprise, there was no sign of the yogi anywhere in the vicinity. He walked towards the rock in the middle of the plateau, sat on it, and wondered what he was going to do next. He did not have to wonder for long as he heard that familiar, deep voice.

"I see you got here all right, Johan. Agni has indeed done a good job."

Startled, Johan looked to his right and was surprised to see the yogi standing next to him, like he had appeared from nowhere. He was extremely thin, and was of average height. He had long hair and a beard, and he was clad only from his waist down. Johan tried to guess his age, but was unsuccessful.

"You are trying to guess my age. Everyone who comes here thinks about my age the first time they see me. You will know my life story someday. Right now we need to train you quickly."

The yogic master came closer to Johan and touched his head. Immediately Johan felt more at peace than he had ever felt before. He felt so close to his master that he wanted to stay like that for as long as he could.

"I am ready to start it right now," Johan replied and sheepishly added, "You can read my mind master?"

"Yes, I can. The dream you had was not really a dream. We did converse when you were asleep," explained the yogi. "Let us evaluate your tennis skills first," the yogi continued. "That will help me evaluate your powers of concentration. I want you to play a match and demonstrate your skills right now."

Johan was a little confused when he heard that the master wanted him to play a tennis match – on the top of a Himalayan peak for that matter. Where would he play, and where was his opponent?

"Johan, close your eyes and it will all be clear," the master instructed. He then went on to place his hand over his head and held him like that for a few minutes.

"You may open your eyes now."

As Johan opened his eyes, he was astonished by what he saw as he was in his tennis attire with a racquet in his hand. Even more astonishing was that there was a tennis court floating above the valley between the peak he was on and the nearest peak. There was a thin layer of fog between him and the tennis court that made the court look like a holographic projection from a far out place. Nevertheless, he slowly walked towards the court and noticed that there was his opponent waiting for him on the other side of the court with a racket and a couple of tennis balls in his hands. They started exchanging some rallies and soon started their match.

While he could not clearly see his opponent's face, he found that his opponent was astonishingly good. He was faster than any player Johan had watched in the pro circuit. He had no shortcomings, and everything about his game was perfect from his forehand to his backhand, volleys, and serves. He was better than Borg, Nadal, or Sampras, and he was even better than his idol Federer, if that was even possible. It was a hopeless proposition for Johan, and he lost the first set 6-0; he had won no points either on his serve or on his opponent's serve. He was humiliated and felt so tired that he could hardly stand straight. He sat down feeling like a lightweight boxer knocked out by the boxing great Mohammad Ali. At that point, the yogi beckoned Johan to come to him.

"You are not focusing, Johan. Now close your eyes and meditate. You need to focus harder," the master advised as he put his hand on Johan's head.

As Johan meditated, he felt the yogic energy from his master penetrating his entire body. He could even feel the negative forces that cluttered his body and mind melting away. He then heard his master asking him to come out of his meditation. He now felt almost weightless and knew he was ready to face any tennis opponent.

The next set was the most thrilling tennis he had ever played. He defended every menacing shot from the other side of the net whether it was a cross court shot or a down the line shot. He attacked his opponent like a ferocious tiger on the prowl for a hapless prey. He stood tall and confident. In spite of all that, he still lost the set. However, the score was very close; 6-7 with a tiebreaker score of 8-10, and he was beckoned by his master again.

"You lost again because your mind is still cluttered. There must be something that still holds you back."

"I don't know. I wanted to win so badly, and I was completely focused. At least I thought that I was completely focused."

"That is where the problem is Johan. You need to cleanse your mind of that desire. You need to remember the verse

2.47.[15] Your focus must be the karma (work) at hand and not the fruits of karma. As long as you do not renounce the fruits of karma, you are not a karma yogi."

The yogi asked him to meditate again as he placed his palm on Johan's head. This time he felt a pain like he was losing something very dear to him as the yogi removed the last vestiges of desire from within Johan. The next set was a breeze for Johan, and he was not bothered by the monstrous serves from his opponent as they looked almost timid. With his focus at the highest level ever possible for a mortal being, the serves which were coming at more than 150 mph seemed a lot slower. They seemed so slow that he had ample time to hit winners out of the high kick serves that his opponent showered on his backhand side. When the set was over he had walked away victorious, winning 6-2 and feeling like he had just played a recreational set with Nick. He was no longer tired and he felt so light that he knew he was ready to acquire the power of levitation.

"This is enough training for today, Johan. Over the next few weeks you will master all the yogic powers from levitation to telepathy. The last power you will master is the power of para kaya pravesha (parallel body experience)".

Johan was humbled by the whole session as he knew he was now on his way to becoming a young yogi. When he turned back to take one final look at his opponent, all he could see was the green valley deep below between the towering peaks. He did not know if the whole experience was just some sort of illusion that the yogi had created, but it really did not matter to him.

---

15 *Bhagavad Gita 2.47:* To karma (work) alone you have the right and never to the fruits of karma. Don't be impelled by the fruits of karma, nor be tempted to withdraw from your karma.

The next few days of training progressed at an amazing speed. Through the power of meditation and yogic focus, he had mastered levitation, telepathy, and the ability to travel at astonishing speeds. Johan was surprised at the speed he had acquired these powers. He knew deep inside that the powers had been literally transferred from his master according to the ancient tradition of guru *parampara*.[16] He wondered who the guru for his master was, reminding him again that he knew nothing about his master's past.

"Can you tell me your past, Maha Yogi? I am burning with curiosity to know how you came here." Johan pleaded.

"Time will come when you are ready to hear my story; this is not the right time for you to know my past." The yogi was again reluctant to reveal his past.

Johan was disappointed by his master's answer. He wanted to ask his master why he had chosen him to be his student. What were the other missions he had in mind for him? Before he could even ask these questions, the yogi answered as if he read Johan's mind.

"There is a spiritual linkage among yogis and future yogis. These linkages are there because of events in past lives. You are here because of things that happened in your past life. All of that will be revealed later."

Johan always knew that the supernatural events he had experienced since his childhood had something to do with his past lives. He had always felt that he had known Kaya from his past life as well. Nevertheless, he was not sure that such things were even remotely possible. But now he was convinced with the Maha Yogi himself revealing the connection.

---

16 *Parampara denotes a succession of teachers and disciples in traditional religions of India such as Hinduism, Buddhism, Jainism, and Sikhism.*

"I will enter your body now, and I want you to take me to Devi Ghat," the yogi instructed Johan. He wanted Johan to learn about the power of Devi Ghat.

Johan stood few feet from his master as the yogi went into a deep meditative state. Within a minute, he could sense his master entering his body. He was not scared this time and was ready to do whatever his master wanted.

"I want you to go down the mountain with the power of levitation," the yogi instructed.

Slowly, Johan lifted himself up with the newly acquired power and moved forward into the space above the valley. He slowly started drifting down as he gradually released his power, and in no time he was standing on the steps of the pond at Devi Ghat.

"Go ahead and drink the sacred water. From now on you have the power to generate energy that you need from the nature that surrounds you," the yogi's voice instructed.

As he sipped the divine water blessed by the Goddess Durga, Johan could feel each and every cell of his body being energized, and within minutes he was a different person. He knew that he was now a true yogi. Drinking the holy water was the final step of initiation becoming a true yogi. The only other thing left to complete in his training was to acquire the power of *para kaya pravesha*, but this could only be mastered once one has been initiated as a yogi. One is not considered a real yogi until one has mastered that special power.

For next few days, Johan practiced the powers he had acquired. He made several trips to Devi Ghat, spoke to his guru only through telepathy and even explored the surrounding mountain peaks. Finally, it was time for him to acquire the power of *para kaya pravesha*. This was the highest yogic power. The yogi asked him to sit down and meditate for an hour, and as he attained the highest state of meditation, the yogi entered Johan's body through his power of soul-migration. In that unique position when the teacher's soul was as close to Johan's as possible, the yogi transferred the ancient mantra to Johan. This was the mantra that when recited at the highest level of meditation allows the yogi to begin his or her soul-migration. The yogi then quietly left Johan's body and re-entered his own body.

But knowing the mantra alone was not enough to acquire that power. Johan had to be unselfish in every way, detached from all aspects of the material world, for him to acquire that special power. When he tried hard to execute that power, he failed miserably. He knew that he could not acquire that power until he had shed the last trace of selfishness from within his heart. The last vestiges of selfish desires that lingered in his mind prevented him from acquiring that last yogic power. Selfishness, he knew, manifested in many ways; he wondered what was that prevented him from acquiring the power. He felt like a failure, a worthless loser; he felt agitated and his anger grew beyond his wildest imagination. He did not realize that the desire to attain the special power itself was the obstacle to his goal. At that time he heard his master's soothing voice which gave him this divine advice:[17]

"There is an unfulfilled desire deep inside you that has given birth to wrath within you. From wrath comes delusion which has robbed your intelligence. A man without intelligence is a man on a path to total destruction."

Perhaps it was the scriptural advice or perhaps it was the soothing voice itself, but Johan immediately felt calm and at

---

17 *Bhagavad Gita 2.63:* From wrath arises delusion; delusion leads to failure of memory which perishes intelligence. Loss of intelligence ensures total destruction.

peace. He felt serene and started meditating again; this time as he meditated, his mind became clearer and was finally rid of all attachments to external world. He felt his desires gone and was free of all sense of "mine" and he had finally reached the true yogic plane.

This time as he recited the mantra, something strange happened. It was the strangest feeling he had ever experienced; it was like he was floating into outer space and he could see himself sitting and meditating. It happened so fast that it took him a while to realize that he was no longer within his own body. For a moment and only for a moment, he felt like a child lost in an unfamiliar place and felt naked and sacred. He then slowly turned and entered his own guru's body. He had finally mastered the power of soul migration.

CHAPTER 18
First Odyssey

There was a long silence as Johan stayed inside his guru's body struggling to find his bearings. Who was he without his physical body and how would he define his existence now that no one other than his guru could even recognize his existence? It all felt very confusing, confusing to the extent that he felt a little scared. The more he thought about the question of existence the more scared he felt and his ultimate fear was that he may never be able to get back to his own body. Within minutes, his fear was gone and was replaced by a strange longing to get back to his body as he discovered that he missed his body immensely, the body he had loved all his life. The more he thought about that strange longing, the more puzzled he became. Now that he was just a spirit unattached to his material body; why would he have such feelings towards his body? It all seemed very illogical to him.

"It is because you are not yet a pure spiritual body." He heard his guru speak comforting him.

"Your soul is still impure. It has the residue from your present life body attached to it and that is what makes you longing for your body," the master explained. That seemed logical to Johan. "Your soul is not pure until you have burnt all your karma in this life. That is when it will depart from your body."

"What is my ultimate karma in this life, Master?" Johan was curious to know the primary reason for existence in this world.

"I will explain that when the time is right. For now, I want you to go back to your body and complete the real cycle of soul migration. Once you have completed the cycle, you are ready to experience its power."

Johan gracefully moved out of his guru's body this time. He looked down at his own body and was eager to reenter it and as he reentered his body, his body shook like there was a mild tremor. He sat up and saw his smiling spiritual master next to him.

"That was not difficult, was it?"

"No, it was not. But it was a strange feeling to be out of my physical body, and I am still amazed how one's soul is attached to a material body."

"Indeed, the power of attachment is the most difficult to overcome, especially attachment to one's own body."

"What do you want me to do now, master? You said I should experience this newly acquired power of soul migration."

"Yes, I want you fly all over this ancient land. I want you to see the wonders as well as the wretchedness that blankets this great land – the land on which the great Buddha once walked."

Johan felt excited as he was confident that he could get in and out of his own body and was now ready to experience the thrill and joy of his newly acquired power. Seeing Johan's excitement, the master had this advice:

"I must warn you about the new power you have just mastered. This power may give you an uncontrollable urge to help others, especially when they are in despair. That urge will take you to places that you never intended to visit. I am worried that you may not be ready to deal with it."

"I am ready for any challenge I might face, Master. I want to soar above the mountains. I want to fly all over the plains from sea to sea," Johan replied as the warning did not dampen his excitement.

"All right, let us start your maiden voyage now. Before we do that, I want to tell you this. Whenever you are in trouble and need help, make three circles on your left palm with your right index finger. That will send me a signal that you are in trouble, and I will immediately send someone to help you."

The yogi then turned north and made a sign with his right hand which looked like he was writing the symbol Om. Within minutes Johan saw a white bird flying towards them from a distant peak; it appeared to be a cross between a mountain eagle and a seagull. It approached them and landed gracefully at his master's feet.

"Johan, this is Mitra. He will be your companion in your voyage. You will enter his body and he will show you all the important places along the holy river Ganga. You may also have a surprise along the way."

The yogi then instructed Mitra to be gentle with Johan. "Mitra, you know the routine. This is not the first time you have guided a soul. I want you to be gentle with Johan. Should he go astray, I want you to follow him until he comes back to you."

Mitra bowed his head in agreement. It was now time for Johan to enter Mitra as he bowed to his guru and sat down to enter the deep meditative state to perform the soul migration. Within a few minutes, he was ready to recite the special mantra which took him away from his body, and he slowly entered Mitra.

It was the same feeling he had earlier when he had entered his guru's body. He felt a sense of excitement with a tinge of nervousness; nervous about the fate of his body when he was gone. He knew it was absurd to be worried about his material body as the great yogi would never do anything to harm him. He was once again astonished at the power of attachment.

As Mitra started flying, Johan could see the peaks of the Himalayas with the visual power of the bird. He marveled at majesty of the mountain peaks and looked back at the peak where the yogi lived which was now far away from him and he felt like a child who was leaving home for school for the first time.

As Mitra glided over the peaks and valleys and descended to the lower levels of the great Himalayan mountain chain, Johan could now see the green forest dotted with pristine streams of water. Mitra went in circles over Devi Ghat where he saw some pilgrims offering prayers on the steps of the pond. Mitra now started flying faster, almost like a super-sonic jet. He flew over the village where Johan and Agni had rested on their earlier journey towards the great yogi.

Mitra was now flying parallel to Bhagirati, the source stream for the sacred river Ganga. The river started getting wider as it entered the plains at the holy city of Haridwar where he could see thousands of pilgrims bathing in the river. He could also see a large statue of Lord Shiva that adored one of the nearby hills. Mitra then made circles around all the temples in the town that made Johan feel spiritually uplifted.

Mitra then flew along the river Ganga to Prayag where Ganga and another important river Yamuna come together.

Johan remembered how he had started his wild quest to find his guru at the banks of the river confluence. Mitra then changed his direction and started flying north along Yamuna. He flew over the Taj Mahal, and in few minutes he was flying over Mathura, the city where Lord Krishna was born. He circled over the temple and was now flying towards Delhi, the capital of India.

As they reached Delhi, Mitra flew over all the important landmarks from Parliament to Delhi Fort to give him an aerial view of that great city. He then turned back and started travelling south east again towards Prayag. From Prayag he rushed towards Varanasi, often considered the holiest place by followers of the Hindu faith. He soared along the Ghats as he witnessed thousands of pilgrims bathing in the holy Ganga. He then circled above the temples and started flying further south. Mitra took a small deviation to fly over Gaya where Buddha had delivered his first sermon. Mitra then flew to Bodh Gaya where Buddha had attained his Enlightenment. He saw the giant statue of sitting Buddha in the city as they travelled further east along the river over the city of Patna, the ancient capital of the Mauryan Empire.

Finally, Mitra flew along the river Ganga as it merged with the mighty river Brahma Putra and it became river *Padma* as it merged with the ocean. Mitra had given Johan a tour of the entire path of the sacred river Ganga; Johan had now experienced the sights of the holy river as no one had ever done before. He felt spiritually energized, but at the same time, he had travelled so fast that he felt dizzy.

"We are not done yet, Johan. I am now going to take you to a place that will have a wonderful surprise for you," Mitra explained.

This was the first time Mitra had ever said anything. Johan was so engrossed in absorbing the majesty of the river Ganga and the temples along his odyssey that he had completely forgotten about the bird.

"What surprise, Mitra?"

"You will know in few hours. I am now going to turn back and fly towards Varanasi. You will know exactly what I am talking about."

Johan got anxious and could not wait to see what the surprise was going to be.

"Did the yogi ask you to do this?"

"Yes, he did. He had told me about this assignment long before you came to him. I was eager to meet you and take you on this journey, Johan."

Johan kept quiet and waited for them to reach Varanasi. As they approached the city of Varanasi, Mitra flew over the city towards the northern outskirts. Johan noticed that the area looked like a large park spanning several hundreds of acres with a big house at the center of the park. The park was lush with several tropical trees, and there was even a small pond at the western edge of the park. There were several smaller houses in the park that were built in a dormitory style. As they got closer, Johan noticed that it was an ashram run by some spiritual organization. Mitra lowered himself and started gliding towards a large banyan tree that was not too far away from the pond.

Mitra was now only a few feet above the ground and Johan noticed a blond haired woman sitting on a stone bench beneath the banyan tree. Johan was shocked and felt dizzy when he realized that it was none other than his mom who was sitting beneath the tree. She was wearing a white sari and was reading a book. Johan got extremely emotional and as the yogi himself had said, the attachment to his present life was too strong even in his existence as a spirit. He was sad that he could not talk to her and that she could not see him. At the same time he was joyous beyond limits that she was alive and well. He asked Mitra to get a little bit closer to her and distract her so that he could look into her eyes.

Mitra went closer and started flapping his wings and making unusual noises to get Nicole's attention. The noise got her attention and she looked at the bird. She was a little surprised to see the bird in the garden as it was a species she had never come across before, neither in India nor in America. It was a mixture of white and brown in color and looked like a cross between a seagull and an eagle. She assumed that it was some exotic mountain bird that rarely visited the plains. To her surprise she felt drawn to the bird and was overcome with uncontrollable desire to hold the bird.

"Come here. Come next to me. Don't be afraid," she said softly trying to coax the bird to come near her.

The bird, as if it understood her, started moving slowly towards her and lifted its face and started staring at Nicole. Nicole was puzzled by the intensity of its stare and was even more surprised at the sudden desire in her to hold the bird.

"Come and sit next to me," Nicole patted on the bench area next to her as Mitra obediently jumped on to the bench and came closer to her.

Nicole looked into the eyes of Mitra and felt close to the bird and wanted to hug it. Even more surprising to her was the urge she had to tell the bird about her story.

"You are probably wondering how I got here, aren't you?" she questioned. Even before she had finished that question she felt very awkward that she was talking to a bird. However, when Mitra nodded his head in agreement whatever uneasiness she had in talking to the bird was quickly erased.

"I was sick for a long time. I was sick to the extent that I did not even know how serious my situation was. I don't know how John and Johan dealt with me. But they were wonderful, and they did everything to keep me happy."

Johan understood everything his mom said. However, that did not explain how she got here in the ashram.

"I remember that day very clearly. My other personality had taken over. She was uncontrollably sad that Junior was no more. It was all in my head; I know that now. She made me leave Dallas, and I was gone in minutes. I landed in London and was soon wandering through Europe from city to city, form hostel to hostel. It was when I was in Rome that I met another traveler, Nadia, who became my friend and brought me here."

Johan wondered how she had come to India from Rome. As if she understood the question, Nicole continued with her story.

"It was not a straight trip from Rome to here. Nadia and I travelled to Tripoli from Rome. They we went east to Cairo and from Cairo we went south to Nairobi. It was in Nairobi that we met our swamiji.[18] When we attended his lecture, we liked it so much that we wanted to join his ashram. Now I am here, and I have never felt so peaceful in my life."

Johan was happy that his mother had finally found peace and happiness. He wondered if she would ever come back to America.

"I am afraid to leave this ashram. I am afraid that if I go outside, I will not be myself again. I will become the confused jumbled soul with multiple personalities. I don't want to go back there again," Nicole added as she wondered why she was telling all this to a bird and looked up into the sky that was now orange with the sun disappearing in the

---

18 *Swamiji refers to a man who has taken the oath of renuncia-*
   tion and has been initiated to a religious monastic order.

horizon. When she looked down to see the bird, she was surprised to see tears in the bird's eyes. She had never seen a bird crying and was overcome with emotions to hug the bird. Instinctively, she bent down to hug Mitra and it was Nicole who had tears in her eyes now.

When she finally released Mitra, Johan was relieved and happy. He was happy that his mother was healthy now and had finally found peace and happiness. He was not sure if he should come back in his real body to see her. At least he had accomplished his original mission, and he was now ready to go back to the Himalayas and join his body. Nicole got up and was ready to walk back to the main building of the ashram.

"It felt really good talking to you. I hope to see you again some time soon," she bid good bye to Mitra and Johan and started walking towards the center of ashram.

Mitra started flying back towards the mountains as Johan was wondering what he was going to do next. He was now feeling anxious to get back to his own body. It was getting dark and the only light was from the moon that lit the land below. They had travelled east for several hours when Johan felt an insurmountable urge to get out of Mitra's body. He was under the influence of an unstoppable force that was pulling him out of Mitra. He looked down and saw a young girl running desperately as if she was afraid for her life. It looked like she was in utmost danger. Johan remembered what the yogi had told him; his new power would compel him to enter bodies that needed help. He was now controlled by that desire to help others, and in no time he had left Mitra and had entered the young girl's body.

CHAPTER 19
Pastor John

Pastor John Midland had traveled more than ten thousand miles to arrive at the crowded city of Lucknow. He was a heavy set man with mild mannerisms who was drawn to India by the stories he had read in the Christian media. It was extremely troubling for him that for a country which held more than a billion people, most were not even aware of Jesus and his message. How could it be that millions of Indians were yet to hear the good news? It troubled him the most that those seemingly nice people were destined to Hell and had no hope of surviving the world's end. Wasn't it time for devoted Christians like himself to bring poor Indians to the Kingdom of God? Wasn't this the whole purpose of God sacrificing his own son?

Pastor John, as he was called, ran a small town congregation in south-east Georgia. His town was a little more than one hundred miles from Atlanta. His church was unique in that it was a successful Jehovah's Witness congregation right in the middle of the Southern Baptist country. He had heard all about the success of the Baptist missionaries in India. Of course, Baptist churches were richer as they had a much larger following than Jehovah's Witness churches. It had bothered him that his church was not involved enough in missionary activities in India. As a devout follower of the JW doctrine, he wanted to bring the poor people of India into his church's fold before Armageddon, which he knew was imminent. He had concluded that it was his moral duty and obligation to do something about it, and he had taken it upon himself to bring the poor in India into the JW fold.

He had studied the culture and religion of India and had found many similarities between the doctrines of JW church and Hinduism. In his mind, Hinduism was nothing more than a corrupted interpretation of God. The teachings he had found inside Hindu religious texts were nothing but distorted interpretations of the Bible, the only inerrant words of God. He found it interesting that Manu, the first man God had created in the Hindu religion and who had authored the laws for the masses, was nothing but a deluded seer. It was laws of Manu that had ordained the terrible behavior of "caste" Hindus towards *Dalits*, the poorest of the Hindu masses. On the other hand, according to Jehovah's witnesses, Jesus, the first man created by God, was full of love and compassion. That irony had struck him the most, and Pastor John was energized to lift the poor in India from the clutches of Manu's indoctrination. He had also concluded that what Hindus called Maya was nothing but the invisible Satan. From everything he had read about India, unending poverty, corruption, and destitute were all due to the dirty work of Satan. Indeed, it was as if the Satan had camped permanently in that nation.

He had also studied the techniques that had been used by the Baptists and Catholic missionaries in proselytizing poor Indians. They had started at the lowest social strata, beginning by promising poor Dalits a better life, whether that meant two square meals a day, building them a house, a school or a clinic. However, often it meant distributing hard cash to the poor, and his other Christian friends found absolutely nothing wrong with that. Anything and every-thing was moral to bring those poor souls to Jesus, even if it meant financing Maoist rebels who were ruthless killers. It was a common belief among many caste Hindus that mis-sionaries financed the Maoist rebels. The rebels were known for cold-blooded killings in the countryside which often caused painful dislocations. Missionaries and their agents considered those dislocations as the necessary evil. In their mind, the more dislocations there were in the society, the more the opportunities for bringing the people of India to Christ. They could not always depend on natural disasters like floods and earthquakes to achieve their goals. The mis-sionary circles had concluded that they had to create their own openings and his friends had told him that Maoists were a very useful force for that purpose. He did not know if the connection between the Maoists and the missionaries was truthful or not, but had decided that he was not going to use any subversive method. He was to do his mission the old fashioned way like any other Jehovah's Witness, by preaching from door to door.

Several years ago, his Baptist friends considered people like him an affront to Christianity and considered Jehovah's Witness a cult. The traditional churches as well as some secular groups considered them an authoritarian group that brain-washed its members. The fact that the Jehovah's Witness refused to accept blood transfusion only reinforced that belief. For this and other reasons, they were always the butt of jokes by comedians that ruled the late night network shows. All this used to infuriate Pastor John, and as a defen-sive move, he often used to quip, "At least we do not have multiple wives like those Mormons."

However, over the past decade relationships with other church groups had improved. Perhaps it was because of the threat to the American Christian culture from outsiders like Muslims, Buddhists, and Hindus. Or perhaps it was because some celebrities had embraced the Jehovah's Witness denomination, which had brought respect to the movement. Baptists did not mind talking to Pastor John once in a while, and he had learned a lot from them about missionary work in India. He had learned that it cost on average around five hundred dollars to convert a Dalit; a majority of that money went to corrupt politicians and various middle men. Thanks to early pioneers, everything about bribing was now institutionalized, and all he had to do was meet an agent in Lucknow to carry out his mission. A network of agents was now firmly established, and the agents handled everything for missionaries, whether it was bribing the officials or funding shady groups like the Maoists.

Pastor John was tired from his long journey from Atlanta to Delhi. He had taken a break in Delhi and stayed with a missionary contact his friends had recommended back in Atlanta. His name was Bill, and he hosted new missionaries like the pastor. Bill was a tall, heavy Indian with a thick mustache. He took care of all the logistics, including dealing with government agencies to handle the paper work. His specialty was helping missionaries whose focus was in Jharkhand, a poor, predominantly rural state that was a few hundred miles east of Delhi. He was part of an organization that had a very secretive structure. He reported to a "Madam" whom he had never met; the Madam only communicated to him through intermediaries. He knew who she was, but he had never dared to mention her name in front of anyone lest he should lose his lucrative business. Within the organization, he was considered the head agent for Jharkhand. Each head agent was assigned a state of the union. In some cases, a state was divided into multiple territories with a head agent assigned to each sub-territory within the state.

A day after he had arrived in Delhi, Pastor John and Bill sat in the veranda of his large house trying to escape from the summer heat. Pastor John was slowly recovering from his jet-lag and had not yet acclimated to the North Indian heat. Even though he was familiar with summer heat as it got very hot and humid back in Georgia, he found the May heat in Delhi almost unbearable.

"Did you get enough rest yesterday?" Bill asked as they both sipped some cool lemonade.

"Yes, I must have slept for almost ten hours. I feel much better today," replied the pastor.

Pastor John was not interested in niceties such as small talk. He was more interested in the details of the next leg of his journey. He had raised more than fifty thousand dollars for his missionary work, and he wanted to make sure that he got enough return for that investment. His immediate interest was to find out more information about the second phase of his journey.

"So, when am I going to visit this village you mentioned over the phone?" Pastor John asked anxiously.

"Don't worry about anything, Pastor. Everything has been arranged. My driver, Jag will take you to Lucknow and drop you in a hotel. Rest in that hotel, and the next day, my guy, Neal, will come and take you to the village," explained Bill, trying to relax the Pastor. This pleased the Pastor immensely as he dreamed about finally building the first JW Kingdom Hall in a Jharkhand village. That would be the first step in weeding out the pagan practices in the village. His body shook involuntarily as he thought how the practice of worshipping idols had flourished across India over the ages. However, it was not too late, and there was still some time left to help those pagans. The Armageddon was still a few years away.

Seeing that the pastor was now relaxed, Bill tried to explain the gains the missionaries and his network had made over the last decade.

"You know, Pastor, for the last ten years, things have really become easy for us. There is easy flow of money from Europe and America, and the media is completely in our hands. We now bring almost a million poor souls a month to Jesus," Bill explained. Seeing that the Pastor was somewhat puzzled, Bill continued to explain.

"Twenty-thirty years ago, it was very difficult to do missionary work in India. Today, thanks to the Madam, things have changed dramatically. We now control most of the politicians and police officers. In the past ten years, she has done more for the Christian cause than the British did in two hundred years," added Bill.

The pastor nodded his head with a seal of approval. It was indeed a very exciting time for the missionaries, and he could not wait to start his journey to Lucknow the next morning.

The journey from Delhi to Lucknow was uneventful. As they entered the center of Lucknow, the Pastor was struck by chaotic traffic and the dirtiness of the city. Lucknow was a very crowded city full of dirty side walks with all sorts of street vendors who were packed in front of stores, selling myriads of goods - clothes, shoes, utensils, and furniture. His driver dropped him at a small hotel in the center of Lucknow city. As he got out of the car with his bag, he looked up to measure the hotel; the establishment was named *Hotel Akash*, and one look told him that it was a two star hotel at best. He did not mind staying there as he was going to be there only for one night. Jag, the driver had told him that Neal would meet him the next morning and had provided him with Neal's cell phone number. He had stored the number in a cell phone that Bill had provided for him in Delhi.

The next morning, he had finished his breakfast and was about to check out when his phone rang. It was Neal informing him that he was on his way to the hotel. Pastor John went hurriedly downstairs with his bag, checked out of the hotel, and waited for Neal in the front lobby. Within a few minutes, a young man with an average build came smiling towards him.

"You must be Pastor John; I am Neal, I'll drive you to the village. The drive should not take more than three hours."

Neal shook the pastor's hand and then took his bag as they walked out of the hotel. As they walked out of the hotel lobby, something made Neal look back and stare at the pastor. He experienced a mild shiver as he looked into the pastor's eyes. It reminded him about something from his past; something he would rather forget.

Pastor John noticed that Neal was driving an old Fiat car which seemed to be at least forty years old. There were no seat belts, and the engine made such a loud noise that it was difficult to carry a conversation. As they drove off from Lucknow further east towards the sate of Jharkhand, the pastor noticed hundreds of shrines in street corners dedicated to local gods. As a Christian and a strict adherent to the Watch Tower edicts, he was appalled by that brazen affront to God Almighty. Disgusted, Pastor John declared in a matter of fact way, "Look at all the idolatry in this land; this country surely has decades of cleansing ahead. Don't you agree, Neal," the Pastor turned to Neal.

For a moment, and only for a moment, the pastor felt a little ashamed for making a harsh statement like that. However, he concluded that God had intended him to make that statement which only strengthened his conviction.

Neal, however, pretended not to hear that statement. The windows were open, and the wind was howling loudly. This, along with the engine's noise, made it almost impossible to hear anything, and it was easy for Neal to ignore the pastor.

Neal appeared to be calm and collected as he seemed to be fully aware of his surroundings; this was only a façade as there was a storm brewing inside his head. At the very moment, Neal was experiencing a flood of wild images in his head, the very images he had desperately avoided over the past five years. There were images of his mother, Father Joseph, and those dreadful nights. Images that were constant staple in his recurring nightmares during his teen years. They were the images of his mother crying, and the continuation of assaults and a sense of guilt and helplessness. It went on for months as the assaults continued and his sense of desperation got worse by the day, and finally it was over. The abuse only ended because of his mother's suicide. But the nightmares never stopped, and it was only after he had entered college that the nightmares stopped. He had overcome this by rejecting humanity as a whole and God in particular as he had concluded that God was nothing but an irrational fantasy. If God existed, how could one explain his mother's suffering night after night?

Neal knew it was dangerous for him to drive anymore. He decided to take a break and rest for a while. Luckily for him, he saw a small tea stall a few hundred yards away where a group of villagers had gathered around the teawala. He stopped his car and parked it on the unpaved shoulder away from the traffic.

"Are you in mood for some tea, Pastor?" Neal inquired.

"Not really. Go ahead and have your tea. I am not much of a tea drinker. I am really a coffee person," John replied.

"We can ask him to make some coffee as well," Neal replied as they got down.

Soon they were sitting on a wooden bench next to the teawala sipping their drinks. Neal looked at the pastor again and saw the same grey eyes. It was the same round pink face, the same hair, and the same pleasant smile. It was like Father Joseph had come back. Neal started to sweat, but he knew very well that it was not from his tea.

"Neal, we are going to spend quite a lot of time together. Perhaps, you can tell me about yourself," encouraged the pastor.

Neal was not in any mood to share his story with the pastor. However, after a while, he decided to open up. He told Pastor John how his father had died in a massive flood when he was only seven years old when his whole village was submerged. He and his mother had lost everything when a missionary group came to help them and take them to a church near Lucknow. The stay in the church was good for few months. However, things got worse after the arrival of Father Joseph who had taken special interest in his mother. His mother wanted to leave but they had no place to go and they were trapped and felt helpless. In the end, his mother could not take it anymore.

He then explained how his mother had died of pneumonia a few years later, which was an outright lie. He left out all the dark parts of his past as he slowly explained his story.

"So, did you go to college?" asked John.

"Yes, I did. I studied history and political science. Unfortunately, there was no job available for someone with that degree. So, I took this job," Neal explained.

Neal paid the teawala a couple of extra rupees as they left the stall. The tea vendor was so pleased that he thanked them profusely.

"Just a couple more hours of driving, Pastor. We will be reaching the village where you can bring those wretched souls to your God", declared Neal as they entered the car and began the next leg of the journey.

CHAPTER 20
God's Plan Gone Awry

It was almost 2 pm when they finally reached *Narang Pur,* a small village deep inside Jharkhand. They had made one more stop for lunch, and Pastor John had slept for the rest of the journey. When they finally reached the village, he felt relaxed and energized; he could hardly hold back his excitement and was eager to meet the village head to begin his God-inspired work. He saw endless possibilities in achieving his life-long dream of bringing God to the millions of poor who were yet to hear the good news. He knew his work was risky as it was bound to disturb the social equilibrium; at times missionary work had even led to fighting and killings among different groups of villagers, but to him someone had to do it, and it was worth the risk.

Narang Pur meant the city of orange groves. This was a misnomer as there were no orange groves anywhere in sight. There were perhaps many orange groves nearby several centuries ago, but all they could see now surrounding the village were marginal farmlands growing what appeared to be wheat.

Neal parked his car beneath a tree just outside the edge of the village as he took out his cell phone and started talking to someone in Hindi. He was on the phone for almost ten minutes while the pastor sat silently waiting for his cue. Neal finally ended his call, closed his flip phone, and opened the door.

"Let's go. Everything is in order." He turned towards the Pastor and smiled.

They both started walking slowly towards the village on an unpaved road with Neal holding a brief case and the Pastor holding his Bible. As they approached the village, Pastor John noticed that the village had two groups of houses. One set of houses were to the east of the village whereas the second set, a smaller group, was to the west of the village. The houses that were to the east were better built, and he noticed one large house at the center of that group. There were fifty to sixty houses in that group. The other set of houses were small huts built with mud walls and thatched roofs while a small open area separated the two groups of houses with two water wells at the center of the field.

"You are wondering why there are two wells in the field, Pastor?" asked Neal.

Before, the pastor could say anything, Neal continued, "The small one is for the Dalits while the larger well which has a much nicer wall is for the rest of the village. The Dalits were not allowed to draw water from the same well as the rest of the village folks as the Dalits were considered untouchable before the practice was outlawed. It is a legacy of that practice," explained Neal.

"I see. That explains the state of those thatched huts," replied the pastor.

"Yes, it does. The Dalits are your people, the ones you are bringing to God. Nevertheless, you need blessing from the village head, Vijay Singh, who lives in that big house before you can do anything in this village." Neal pointed towards the large house on the good side of the village.

As soon as they reached the house, a servant opened the door and hurriedly let them in, immediately closed the door behind the visitors. He then took them to a room that was on the side of the entrance and asked them to sit down on the chairs that surrounded a table. It appeared like the room where Vijay Singh did all of his business transactions.

Vijay Singh, a big, hairy man with a large mustache, sat on one side of the table and asked the visitors to sit opposite him as Neal and the pastor had not taken their seats. He smiled at the visitors and waited for them to initiate the transaction. Neal could see a sense of great anticipation in Mr. Singh's eyes.

"Mr. Singh, this is Pastor John who is here to build a small church for the Dalits in your village. In return for your blessings, we have this token of appreciation for you," Neal opened the top of a small brief case as he placed it on the table.

Mr. Singh gave an approving look as he saw Indian Rupees neatly stacked in the brief case.

"How much money is there?" enquired Mr. Singh wanting to make sure that his terms were met.

"There is exactly half a million rupees as you requested. If you are happy with that, we can shake hands and the two of us will go to the Dalit side and take care of the rest of the business," Neal replied as he was anxious to close the transaction.

Nevertheless, deep in his heart, Neal loathed the next phase of his mission. He knew an ancient culture and heritage was going to be assaulted with the Dalit community divided for generations. They would be told that their beliefs were inferior to Christianity and they were going to be brainwashed to hate their ancestral faith with vengeance. Not all Dalits were going accept Jesus and those who did not and those who did would fight for generations. There would be riots and fights which the media men, bribed by the agents of missionaries, would color it as religious violence. Nor was this march of conversion going to alter the life of the poor Dalits. If anything, it was going to add more misery to them. But in the supermarket for Dalit souls, where winning market share was of utmost importance, Neal knew that none of that really mattered to missionaries like Pastor John. This truly pricked his conscience, and he hated himself for being an agent in the supermarket for souls.

Vijay Singh smiled back and nodded his head as he closed the briefcase and got up to shake hands with the visitors. Right at this time, there was a screeching sound of a vehicle coming to a sudden stop. They could hear the vehicle door slam and the footsteps of a man walking towards the front door. Next was the loud bang along with a verbal demand to open the door. As if he recognized the voice, a servant came running to open the door and let a young handsome man in who immediately stormed into the room where Neal and Mr. Singh were about to close their business transaction.

The young man looked very agitated and glanced disgustingly at both Neal and the pastor. He then turned towards Mr. Singh with an even more disgust on his face.

"How could you do this, Dad? We had discussed this last week when I was here, and you had agreed not to go along with this evil plan," the young man protested who was visibly upset and angry.

"Calm down, Vipin. No harm is done letting these people carry out their mission. Moreover, don't you love the smell of these fresh bills?" He opened the briefcase and pointed at the bills with a sly grin on his face. No one said anything for the next few seconds as the young man tried to gather his composure and struggled to put his thoughts into words.

"You want to refuse Goddess Lakshmi[19]?" Vijay Singh asked, trying to exploit the cultural angle.

"You cannot play that game with me, Dad. If you are going to go ahead with the conversion thing, I am going to call my friends, and there is going to be a riot." Vipin gave a terse warning. He was determined to stop Pastor John's plan. Vipin belonged to a local branch of a Nationalistic group that felt that their faith and culture were under attack by the missionaries.

Pastor John was terribly perturbed by what had just transpired. He was witnessing his whole plan crumbling in front of his own eyes, which shook him thoroughly, and he tried to look away through the window.

Mathew 10.34 came to his mind where Jesus himself had said that *"Do not think that I came to bring peace on the earth; I did not come to bring peace, but a sword. For I came to set a man against his father, and a daughter against her mother, and a daughter-in-law against her mother-in-law; and a man's enemies will be the members of his household…"*

It was incomprehensible for him that bringing dignity to a people who were oppressed by their own neighbors was considered an evil plan. What was really evil about spreading the words of Gospel to the poor people of India?

Neal sensed that it was not safe for him and the pastor to stay in that village any longer. He hurriedly closed the briefcase and apologized to the younger Singh.

"We are sorry, Vipin-ji[20]. If that is the way you feel, we will simply leave this place. I am sorry it did not work out

---

19 *Lakshmi is Goddess of wealth, and refusing money, even if it is illicit, is considered disrespectful to the Goddess by many.*

20 *Adding "ji" at the end of a name is considered a sign of respect.*

Mr. Singh," he politely apologized and signaled to the pastor to get ready to leave.

It was an awkward situation as the two left Vijay Singh's house with the elder Singh showing extreme sadness with the thought of half a million rupees walking away from him.

When they got back to their car that was parked at the edge of the village, Pastor John looked very disappointed as all of his plans had gone awry, and it had happened so fast that he felt dizzy. They both sat in the car in complete silence wondering about their next step. Finally, when Neal was about to start his car, he saw a middle aged man, who appeared to be a poor Dalit, with a teenage girl walking hurriedly towards them. Neal lowered the window to find out what the man wanted.

"Sir, I saw that you were not coming to our side of the village, so I came quickly to ask for a favor," the man with torn garments asked politely. His daughter, who had big bright eyes, stood a few steps behind him.

"What do you want?" asked Neal impatiently.

"Sir, I am a poor man with five children, and I cannot afford to buy the food we need or get my daughter married off," replied the poor man.

Neal did not want to say anything; indeed, he was not sure what the man wanted. He wondered if he was going to ask for few rupee bills.

"I want you to take my daughter with you and you can take her to your church. All I ask for is five thousand rupees that will help me buy a cow which would be a great help for my family," the poor man explained.

Neal was tired and was in no mood to get involved in transporting a young girl from a village in Jharkhand to Delhi. He had a suspicion that it could only bring more trouble. Nevertheless, he turned to the pastor to get his opinion. Pastor John had not followed any of the conversation as it was completely in Hindi. When Neal translated the poor man's request, Pastor John felt moved and agreed to take her to his main church in Delhi. Neal gave five thousand rupees to the poor man who was extremely happy to receive the money. The girl got herself into the back seat with a small bag in her hand as her father closed the door.

The girl was frightened and sad to leave her childhood village, but she had no choice as the only way she could help her family was to agree to what her father had just arranged. She had recently lost her mother due to a grave illness. She hoped that the money would at least help her four younger brothers and sisters. She knew that her mother would have never agreed to the transaction her father had just completed, but she consoled herself by saying it was her fate and her past karma. She tried her hardest to control her tears as her father slowly started walking away from the car. Neal started the car and started driving slowly on the unpaved road until he reached the asphalt road. As soon as he reached the asphalt road, he shifted the gear and started accelerating with the hope of reaching Lucknow before it was too late in the evening.

CHAPTER 21

Saving a Soul

Neal was depressed that his mission was an utter failure and kept focused on his driving as they drove towards Lucknow. He was extremely disappointed that the trip had turned out to be a failure; his disappointment, however, was nothing compared to that of Pastor John. The pastor's dream of helping the poor and bringing them into his church was now shattered. He did not know what to do next, and his only option was to go back to Delhi and consult his agent Bill to come up with an alternate plan. He stared at the vast wheat fields not saying much to Neal as the car raced along the outdated highway. Neal was disappointed that he had lost a big commission opportunity, and he hoped that he could soon forget the mission and move on to his next venture when he suddenly thought about the girl.

He looked into his rear view mirror to see what the girl was doing in the back seat. She had turned to the side with her hands clasped around her knees with a frightened look on her sad face. Her eyes were red which indicated that she was continuously sobbing. He could sense that she was hungry and tired, probably a daily routine for her.

"Can we stop at the next tea stall?" asked the pastor as he wanted to stretch his legs and get some fresh air.

"That is what I had in mind as well, and we will just do that. I am getting a headache, and I really need some hot tea. I think that the girl is hungry too. We should get her something to eat," Neal replied as he was more than happy to oblige.

When they finally made a stop at the tea stall, Neal asked the girl if she wanted anything to eat. The girl, who was still scared and confused, kept to herself in the backseat staring at the car floor mat and refused to answer.

"It is all right; we will not hurt you in any way. Would you like some bread to eat?" asked Neal again this time his tone was much softer as he tried to put her at ease.

The girl finally nodded her head signaling her willingness to get out and eat something for it was too much for her to miss an opportunity to have a decent meal.

As she sat on the bench eating a piece of bread and drinking tea, Neal decided to find out more about her.

"What is your name? How old are you?" He tried to get the girl to say something as she had not spoken a single word since they had left the village. The girl did not say anything as she was too scared and had no idea where those two strangers were taking her.

"It's all right, you can at least tell us your name," Neal coaxed her.

"Neelu," the girl replied in a very soft voice afraid that Neal would get angry if she refused to talk.

Neelu looked like she was no more than fourteen years old with a frail body and shabby clothes covering her. Anyone could see that she had had a rough life so far; there was never a night when she had gone to sleep without feeling hungry. Unfortunately, she was just one of millions of children caught in the lowest rung of the frozen and outdated social ladder.

Neal looked at Pastor John who was now sitting next to him and drinking sweet tea. He looked so comfortable in that position that it seemed the pastor was completely acclimated to tea culture. As Neal looked at the pastor's profile, his body shook again. He saw Father John sitting next to him and he started perspiring. "Please, help me God, I do not want to relive those nights," Neal prayed silently, terrified at the thought of losing control of his mind. He rubbed his eyes and lowered his head as he tried to control his troubled mind.

"I don't want to go back to that time," he murmured again in Hindi; this time the words came out of his mouth subconsciously.

"What are you saying? Did you say something to me?" The pastor sounded concerned.

"My headache is not helping me. I think we should stop in a hotel or a guest house on the way to Lucknow. I do not want to drive for a long time with my splitting headache," Neal explained.

"No problem, your health and our safety is more important. There is no reason to hurry back to Lucknow," the pastor said approvingly. Moreover, he was dejected that his plan had unexpectedly gone awry; he had to calm down and think about his backup plan.

Neal paid the vendor several rupee bills that included a handsome tip and they were on the road again. They had travelled for another ten miles or so when Neal started slowing the car and turned left to a small side road, and they kept travelling another two miles or so on the side road until they approached the front of a small building. Pastor John looked at the board that read "District Guest House" in English. He knew that they were going to rest in that building for the night. It appeared to be a guest house for government employees. Neal asked Neelu and the pastor to stay in the car and went inside the building.

Pastor John looked at the sky and noticed that it was turning orange, and he knew that it was going to be dark within the next half an hour. He was in the mood for some good sleep as he was tired from all the travel. He looked at Neelu who had a blank look on her face; he could sense that her mind was not in the present, perhaps she was thinking about her siblings back in the village. She had the most beautiful eyes he had ever seen; they were dark that were perfectly shaped like lotus petals. They were also the most innocent eyes he had ever witnessed, and he took some solace that at least his trip was not a complete waste and that he was doing something good. Neelu was going to have a life to look forward to and never had to worry about her next meal again. He only wished that he could help more children like her.

When Neal came back from the building, he did not look very happy and was fuming as he opened the door.

"There is a new caretaker now, and I tell you, he is some bureaucrat," Neal blurted out. "He refuses to give us rooms, and even refuses to take a handsome bribe. Some Mahatma he is," Neal could not hold back his sarcasm with his not so oblique reference to Mahatma Gandhi.

"So, we cannot stay here?" the pastor wanted to know and he sounded a bit concerned knowing Neal's state.

"No, we are going to stay here. He is letting us stay in the hall downstairs. He is arranging three makeshift beds for us," Neal replied, still upset that the caretaker had not cooperated with his plan.

Neal, Neelu and the pastor went inside the building and had finally settled in their beds. The night had finally fallen on all of North Indian plains, and the only illumination outside was the abundant moonlight as it was just two days before the full moon day.

Within a few minutes, Neelu was fast asleep and Pastor John, who was extremely tired was ready to call it a day as well. Neal was in no mood to sleep, however, and he took out a bottle of Johnny Walker from his bag and offered the whisky to the pastor. The pastor politely refused, and it was now his turn to fall into a deep sleep. Neal sat at the edge of his bed slowly sipping the whiskey doing his best to fight the demons; the demons that had ruined his teenage years. He was scared and lonely, and he cried silently, wondering why this was happening to him just when he had convinced himself that he was free of those nightmares. He finally felt relieved as he started calming down, and before he knew it he had fallen asleep.

Suddenly, Neal was woken by the harsh sound of pea-cocks, and he did not know why the birds were making so much noise. Perhaps, it was a mating call or perhaps they were being attacked by an owl but that was one bird noise that drove Neal insane. Irritated, Neal sat up, shook his head, and looked out through the window to calm down. He watched the clouds as they periodically kept covering the moon which made the room frighteningly dark. He waited for the next break in clouds to see the time on his wrist watch and noticed that it was past midnight.

The clouds had completely covered the moon, and it was pitch dark again when Neal started hearing the sound of drums. It was the music that he had heard as a child, the music from his childhood village that represented Lord Shiva doing his cosmic dance. It got louder and louder and then gradually moved to the background as the whole room became dead silent when he heard the frightening footsteps; the footsteps of Father Joseph coming to his room. There he was, the bulky man, trying to force himself as his mother tried to push him back. He could hear the loud slap as his mother kept weeping. Neal was afraid that Father Joseph would mortally hurt him; he curled himself inside the blanket and covered his ears and tried his best to hold back his cry. He tried hard not to hear his mother's suffering; the feeling of helplessness drained his strength as he felt ashamed and worthless. The scenes kept repeating like a vicious circle in his head, becoming increasingly painful every time the scene was played out in his confused head when he could not take it anymore and started screaming.

The sudden screaming woke up both the pastor and Neelu, and Pastor John walked to Neal trying to calm him down. When the pastor came near Neal, he pushed him back and started screaming again.

"You killed my mother, I am going to make you pay for it," Neal jumped on the pastor and tried to choke him as the pastor tried to fight him back not knowing what had suddenly come over Neal.

Pastor John was completely taken aback and had no idea why Neal was behaving like that. He only hoped that he could calm him down somehow but Neal was like a mad man possessed by a monster who would not stop; he kept trying to grab the pastor and pin him down. But the pastor was too heavy for Neal to pin him down, and the failure to do so made him even angrier; he went back to his bed and started sobbing confusedly about his state of mind. He was getting angry and he was terrified at the same time and tried to pull his hair to calm himself down.

Neelu was terrified with everything that was unfolding, and she sat silently on her bed wondering what she should do while the pastor struggled to come up with a plan to calm down Neal. Even his life long experience in helping troubled and confused souls was useless at that moment. Unable to come up with a plan, Pastor John sat next to Neal and tied to calm him down by putting is arm around Neal's shoulder. He tried to gently squeeze him as a way of assuring him. That was, perhaps, a grave mistake.

Then the unthinkable happened. It happened so fast that Neelu was rendered motionless for a minute. Neal had drawn a knife from his bag and had attacked the pastor. He had jumped and stabbed the pastor with such a lightening speed that the pastor had no time to defend himself and was down in a minute as Neal kept stabbing him while continuously sobbing at the same time.

Pastor John, who had come to India to bring poor Dalits to his church, was now a victim of the sins committed by a fellow priest. Perhaps, the Yogi was right when he had mentioned to Johan that all our past karmas are inter-connected. The sad part was that Pastor John had paid the dues for the sins committed by Father Joseph who was indeed an evil abuser of authority.

Neelu realized right at that moment that her own life could be in grave danger and started to run towards the door. She was nervous and was shaking uncontrollably as she tried to unlock the door. The heavy padlock that was made of cast iron made it difficult to open the door and she looked back nervously to see what Neal was doing. Her heart started beating so fast that she felt like she was going to collapse as she realized that Neal had gotten up and started walking towards her.

As Neal walked towards Neelu, she no longer looked like the frightened fourteen year old teenager. Instead what he saw standing in front of him was a plump woman with a stern look on her face. Indeed, it was the second person whom he wanted to erase from his mind, the caretaker at the church who was an accomplice in Father Joseph's atrocity towards his mother. He ran towards her and grabbed her arm with his left palm. When Neelu saw that Neal still had the sharp knife that was dripping in blood in his hand she started crying and tried her best to free herself from his iron grip. Not knowing what to do, she closed her eyes and started praying to Goddess Durga, the Goddess who had protected her people over the centuries in times of crisis.

It was at this point Neelu felt a large bolt, like a surge of several thousand volts of electricity, enter her body. She felt like she was going to have a heart attack or a seizure. To her astonishment, the feeling did not last very long. Suddenly, she felt like she was stronger than ever and was ready to defend her life. To her delight, she was able to push Neal back and free herself from his grip. But Neal was persistent and started charging towards her with his bloody knife. Neelu stopped her attacker, and the two started wrestling while all the while she felt like someone else was controlling her body. She wondered if it was a divine force sent by Goddess Durga to protect her. The wrestling was intense when finally in her attempt to stop Neal she had stabbed him as Neal crumbled to the floor.

"Do not worry; let us get out this place." Neelu heard a voice that seemed to come from within her which frightened her. Nevertheless, she started walking towards the door like some sort of robot controlled by a software program.

She started running into the forest that was a few hundred yards from the back of the guest house, hoping no one would trace her path. She felt lucky that the keeper of the guest house had not really seen her and would have trouble identifying her. She kept thinking about what might happen next and was scared that the police might arrest her for the two deaths. Understandably, she was less bothered by that as she was more concerned about what was going on inside her own body. The voice she had heard just moments before, where did it really come from? She tried to convince herself that it was all within her own head. She wondered if she was hallucinating or if she was possessed by some spirit. She thought about that voice again and remembered that it was very assuring. She felt safe, and she was now convinced that she was possessed by another helpful soul. It was not something unknown to her as she had witnessed many people in her village often being possessed by souls from the past. She was curious to know who was the co-habitant in her body and garnered enough courage to ask him that.

"Who are you, and why have you entered my body," she queried silently.

"My name is Johan. There is nothing for you to worry about, Neelu. I will make sure that you are safe," the voice from within replied.

By the yogic power that Johan had recently acquired he instantly knew who she was and about everything that had transpired in her life over the past few weeks. Just like the yogi had told him, the moment he had entered Neelu's body, all the knowledge and memory that was in her brain was accessible to Johan as well. Johan felt excited and thought that it was more thrilling than the earlier transmigration.

Neelu felt magical as she heard that assurance. It was as if all her worries were gone, and she had never felt so happy in her life. She felt like she was born again, and she was indeed sure that Goddess Durga Herself had sent Johan to save her.

CHAPTER 22
Neelu is Born Again

Neelu was relieved and kept running blindly in the dark through the woods as fast as she could until she came into an open area surrounded by wheat fields. She ignored the pain caused by the sharp pebbles she occasionally stepped on. She was surprised that she was not afraid any more, and she was now comfortable with her companion Johan and even wanted to engage him in a conversation. Just those few minutes of companionship had made her feel like Johan was her brother; perhaps because of the closeness of their souls. Johan could feel the closeness as well, and felt like she was his little sister. She kept asking Johan why he was lost in space and if he was someone from the past who had lived in her village generations ago. When Johan laughed and told her that he was not lost and was indeed from the present and he was truly happy to be with her, she laughed along with him. The dialogue that continued within her head was her way of feeling secure and keeping herself energized. She had walked for almost six miles when she realized that she was coming close to a rural road. She felt relieved as her feet were in extreme pain with minor cuts from all the running she had done barefoot. She hoped that the paved road would be kinder on her tender feet. Neelu had travelled one more mile on the paved street when she noticed some lights not too far away.

"Let us walk towards those lights. It looks like a small village," guided Johan.

This time she started walking briskly, still a little nervous that police might come after her.

"We will find someone who can help you. I want to make sure that you get back to your family safe and sound," Johan tried to make her feel happy.

Neelu did not like what Johan had just uttered. Instead of being a happy assurance, those words seemed like harsh words of punishment. There was no point in going back to her family in the village; there was every chance that her father would sell her to anyone who would pay him some money, however meager it was, as long as it was enough for him to buy some local drinks. That would be like going back to hell again she thought. There was nothing enticing about her home, the perennial hunger, and the obscene poverty she had endured all her life.

She could not help but start crying as tears started rolling down her cheeks, and Johan quickly realized what was going on as he could read her mind.

"Do not worry Neelu, something will come up, and you will finally have happiness in life," he assured her again.

Neelu stopped crying as she recalled that all the crying she had done in her life had never done her any good. She, however, hoped that it would be different this time. Not surprisingly, hope itself was an unknown feeling for her and she was still worried about her fate. Could Johan really help her and change her life, she wondered. Or would she end up in a jail and suffer police abuse and brutality? She had heard horror stories about how police had mistreated poor people back in her village. She had grown up believing that police were not trustworthy.

By now they were almost at the edge of the village and Johan noticed that they were standing in front of a temple. Neelu read the board which stated that it was a Lord Krishna temple. The time was around five in the morning and the temple doors were already open. There were already several people inside the temple who were quietly meditating in front of Lord Krishna's image.

Johan encouraged Neelu to go inside. As they went inside, Neelu observed that there was no priest in the temple. It was as if it was a temple run by the devotees. Devotees were quietly making their offerings, whether they were flowers, fruits, or food. They would silently pray in front of the image of Lord Krishna and would go back in the hall and sit quietly either meditating or repeating some sacred mantra in their own mind.

Johan was, however, more interested in finding someone who could help Neelu. He tried to look around and see if there was anyone who looked like a good prospect for taking care of Neelu. As he scanned the hall, he noticed a well dressed woman in red sari sitting in front of the hall and praying with at most devotion. Sitting next to her was her middle aged husband. Johan quickly realized that they were an affluent couple and would make excellent care takers for Neelu.

"Let us go and sit close to that lady in the red sari," Johan instructed Neelu. Neelu sensed that he was indeed planning something and felt a mild sense of excitement. She did not want to get too excited, however. She closed her eyes and started praying to Krishna asking Him to bring an end to her misery.

The lady was done with her prayers and opened her eyes. She noticed the young girl sitting close by and was curious to know who the girl was as she had not seen the girl before. From her clothes and appearance she guessed that she was from a poor background, perhaps a Dalit. For some unknown reason she kept looking at Neelu as if there was some unexplained relationship between her and the young woman.

"Neelu, I am going to leave your body. I will get back to you once my mission is accomplished. Don't be scared, and I will be back soon," Johan warned.

Within moments, Neelu could feel that there as no one else inside of her. She felt sad and lonely and was fearful. She was fearful that something terrible could happen to her like police walking inside the temple looking for her. She tried to stay calm and focused on her prayer.

Suddenly, Neelu noticed that the lady next to her shook her body as if she had a big jolt and she immediately realized that Johan had entered her body. Although she had no idea why he had done that, she felt happy that he was still in the vicinity.

The lady was in great shock and had no idea what was happening to her as there was big surge of electricity go through her. She started praying again and in few minutes felt at ease as her body stabilized. Johan felt terrible that he had made an awkward entry into her body.

"I am sorry, I did not mean to give you a jolt like that," he apologized.

His apology only startled the lady even more and she wondered what was going on inside her body. First, it was the unbearable jolt and now it was the voice in her head. Am I going insane, she wondered? She had indeed been very upset for the last few days. She had just returned from a pilgrimage from Mathura, the birth place of Lord Krishna. Every time she visited Mathura, it pained her to see how a brutal seventeenth century Muslim ruler had torn down a part of the temple and erected a Mosque in its place. That was injustice she could never endure and it always took several days of praying to calm herself down. She was now worried that this time she had really gone insane thinking too much about that historical wrong.

"You are doing fine. There is nothing wrong with you. I have been sent to you by Lord Krishna to talk to you," Johan tried to calm the lady.

That was too much for the lady and she almost fainted. She, however, garnered enough strength to ask some questions.

"Why has Krishna sent you? Has He finally heard my prayers? I have been begging for a child for so many years," she was excited and at the same time she was complaining.

"Indeed, He has heard your message. Do you see that girl next to you? Her name is Neelu. She is an Orphan, and Krishna wants you to adopt her," Johan proclaimed.

The lady looked at Neelu, and she had a strange but almost instant reaction. She knew it was unwarranted, but as if out of centuries of conditioning the thoughts came out subconsciously.

"She looks like a Dalit," she blurted and within seconds she knew she had sinned. As a devotee of Krishna who had studied Bhagavad-Gita in-depth she knew her thoughts were impure, and she immediately felt ashamed and asked Krishna for forgiveness. Tears started rolling on her cheeks.

Her husband who was next to her noticed the tears and got worried. He put his arms over her shoulder and quietly whispered in her ears.

"Are you alright? Are you not feeling well?"

She shook her head indicating she was doing fine. She had an immediate worry, however.

"What about my husband. Will he agree to adopt a Dalit girl?" she wondered.

"Do not worry. I will take care of that. You just whisper in his ears that you want to adopt Neelu. Tell him she is a gift from Krishna," Johan advised her as he quickly left her.

The woman waited for few moments, garnered enough courage and leaned towards her husband.

"You see that pretty girl next to me? I want to adopt her. She is a gift from Krishna," she whispered in his ears.

Within a fraction of a second of her whispering, Johan had entered the man's body. The man repeatedly heard Johan gently urging him to heed the words of his wife.

"I have come to you from Krishna. He wants you to adopt Neelu and take good care of her," Johan repeated these words like he was chanting a holy mantra.

That was unnecessary though as the man was delighted to see that his wife was willing to adopt Neelu. He had indeed approached his wife about the possibility of adoption in the past without much success. The sudden change of heart in his wife pleased him immensely and he whispered back "yes" in his wife's ears with a big grin on his face.

While this exchange was going on Johan had quickly reentered Neelu's body and had explained to her that the couple were going to adopt her.

"They will take you to the government office where they will ask you about your past. Tell the government people that you do not remember anything other than your name. That way, the couple will be able to adopt you without any hassle," Johan advised Neelu.

The couple got up and slowly walked towards Neelu. The woman took Neelu's hand and asked her to get up. There was no need for any words to be exchanged as they all knew what was happening. It was the Lord's plan and the three of them walked out of the temple towards the gate. As the three of them stood near the gate the man looked at Neelu and explained their intentions.

"We want to take you home. We want you to be our daughter. Is that all right with you?" the man asked Neelu.

Neelu nodded her head in agreement as she looked at the brand new day that was about to shine on her life. She knew that all her troubles were going to be distant memory soon and, indeed, she was indeed born again.

Out of nowhere, Mitra flew in and sat on the gate and Johan knew that it was time for him to go. His mission was accomplished, and he felt extremely happy that he had made good use of his newly acquired powers. He quietly left Neelu without saying any word. Neelu felt the emptiness inside her again and started crying. She did not know if it was because she was sad that Johan was gone or because she had finally found a loving home. As if by instinct, she hugged the woman like a child finding her long lost mother.

CHAPTER 23
My Migraine

Several months had passed since my last trip to India, and I had not heard from Johan and was beginning to wonder if he would ever tell me the rest of his amazing story. When we parted in Chicago, he had told me his story up to the point where he had gotten back to the yogi after having saved Neelu. Apparently, Mitra had kept following him like a faithful friend, and Johan had gotten back to Mitra, who had taken him back to the yogi. Once he had reached the yogi, he was back in his own body and was eager to go back to America as Johan missed Kaya and his other friends. The yogi had explained to him that his mission was not over; the reason he had wanted Johan to come to the Himalayas was for a different mission that was far more dangerous and more involved than finding his mother. Johan had agreed to do that and had promised the yogi that he would come back to the Himalayas soon but only after spending time with his friends.

On his way back to America, Johan had met Mr. Rao, and had donated money to a school that Mr. Rao had built for underprivileged children. The school took care of all the needs of poor children including clothing, books, and daily meals and had provided a loving environment where poor children could nourish their God-given talents. Mr. Rao had built that school in memory of his wife, who had been killed during a terrorist attack in Delhi around Diwali when she had gone to a market place to do some shopping with her friends. Mr. Rao's dream was to make his school an example for other rich people in India to adopt the right vision of Dharma.

I was hoping that Johan would get in touch with me soon to tell me about his next adventure as I was completely spellbound by his story. Furthermore, I was immensely curious about his next task, especially after the yogi had told Johan that it was a dangerous mission. To my great disappointment, I did not hear from Johan for several months.

It was one of those USTA tennis tournaments when I was driving my son to the town of Waco which is about one hundred miles south of Dallas. We had arrived the previous night and were staying at the Fairfield Inn North which was close to McLennan County College, his tournament site. My son had won his first match in the morning and had started his second match soon after we had finished a quick lunch in a nearby sandwich place. It was a perfect day for tennis as it was neither too hot nor too cold and I stood close to the court where he was playing enjoying the match. There was nothing unusual about that day and the match progressed as I had anticipated with both the players holding their serve in the first eight games.

However, all that changed in a matter of minutes. Without any warning, my head started aching, and I could sense that I was going to have a severe migraine. My heart began to beat fast, and I started feeling dizzy. I immediately knew that something was wrong with my body and felt alarmed. I wanted to go back to my room and rest as soon as possible; yet I hesitated as my son's match was not yet over. I was reluctant to return to the hotel as I had to make arrangements for him to get back to the hotel before I drove off in my car. I gingerly walked to Mr. Chan near another court, trying my best to put on a normal smile, where he was watching his son Lawrence play his match. Lawrence and my son Rohith were friends who went to the same school in Plano, and they had been close friends since elementary school. I told Mr. Chan about my migraine and asked him to bring back my son to the hotel room after the match.

Having made those arrangements, I slowly got into my car and carefully drove along Lake Shore Drive back to my hotel and jumped into the bed as soon as I was in my room. As I was beginning to fall asleep, I heard a strange humming noise in my head which almost frightened me. Thankfully, the noise died after few minutes and there was a deafening silence. From nowhere, I heard a very familiar voice; it was Johan's voice. He was now ready to narrate the next phase of his story.

CHAPTER 24
Coma Mystery

Kaya was happy beyond limits that Johan had come back from India sooner than she had ever imagined. There were too many stories she had read in the media recently about young men and women running into trouble in foreign countries that had kept her sleepless many a night. She was also relieved that he had finally met his mother and had a closure to that chapter in his life. Strangely enough, Johan had not talked much about the yogi himself, and his reluctance to discuss his Himalayan journey puzzled her tremendously. She wondered why Johan was not talking about it and was curious if there was something secretive about his journey that he did not want to reveal. What bothered her was the thought that Johan would keep a secret from her.

Although Johan had told Kaya and everyone else that he had finally met his mother in an ashram near Varanasi, he had not revealed to anyone the yogic powers he had acquired nor anything about the incredible odyssey of his with Mitra that had taken him to his mother. He was particularly sensitive about revealing his power of soul-migration and the ability to enter another body as he was not sure how Kaya and others would react. He assumed that they would not believe his story and decided not to divulge that power to anyone. Moreover, he had a deep anxiety about that secret; an anxiety that came along with the power of soul-migration. The side effect was that of the tendency to jump into another body involuntarily when he sensed trouble as in the case of Neelu. After non-stop debates within himself, he had decided not to reveal that side affect to Kaya as it was sure to alarm her. But he also knew that not revealing his yogic powers was not a wise thing to do as he firmly believed that there should not be secrets among close friends. Finally, after thoughtful deliberation, he decided that he had to tell his friends about his yogic powers and his incredible journey that had taken him to the yogi. He would first tell Kaya about his story and later he would tell Nick and PK.

It was Saturday morning and everything seemed perfect; the sky was blue and the temperature was mild, and it seemed like a perfect time for him to tell Kaya about everything. A long drive down along the coast would be the perfect setting for him to tell his story, and Johan decided to drive down to Carmel with Kaya, confident that the long drive would provide him the opportune moment to divulge his secrets.

Johan decided to travel on Route 17 to Santa Cruz and later travelled on 1 South towards Carmel. Not surprisingly, Kaya also thought that the long drive would give her the right opportunity to bring up the topic of Johan's India journey. For the first thirty minutes of the drive, neither Johan nor Kaya spoke much, and once they had crossed Santa Cruz, Kaya decided to bring up the topic of Johan's trip.

"Johan, is there something about your trip that you haven't told me? I have this nagging feeling that you are not telling me everything." She gingerly broached the topic.

Johan, thoughtful that he had to approach his answer the right way lest he should make her feel betrayed, remained silent for a few seconds searching for the right words.

"Well, I have not told you everything as I was not sure that anyone, even you, would believe my story. It is too incredible, too fantastic, and there are too many aspects in my story that go beyond the limits of ordinary science which may lead someone to conclude that I am simply crazy."

"I believe you, Johan, however fantastic your story is. I am not going to call you crazy. To be honest, I can't wait to hear the details of your journey, and the mystery is killing me. Please don't make me wait any longer."

For the rest of their drive, Johan narrated his whole journey to India – his travel to Prayag, his encounter with Agni and how Agni had helped him reach the great yogi at the top of that secret peak in the high Himalayan mountains. He told her about the ancient powers he had mastered – the power of telepathy, the power of soul migration or *Parakaya Pravesha.* Finally, he narrated the incredible journey that he made as a spirit inside Mitra - the mysterious bird who had become his friend, and how he had finally met his mother. He then stopped his narration as he started thinking about his mother and felt relieved that she had finally found a place where she had finally found happiness.

Kaya sensed that Johan was relieved, and she held his hand and gave him a mild squeeze. It was as if she was congratulating Johan for a successful trip and at the same time, telling him that she understood his emotional status. More than that, she was happy that he had finally found a closure on his mother's whereabouts and that his mother had finally found solace and happiness. The lack of closure would had been a permanent fault in Johan's emotional landscape.

"Do you believe my story, Kaya? You don't think that I am making up some fantastic story or that I am crazy or I am of out of my mind?"

"Of course not; I do believe everything you told me, and I believe that soul and body are two distinct entities with the soul being the permanent one. I have told you many times that I have witnessed many supernatural events during the visits to my grandma's house at the reservation, and your story is not fantastic at all."

By that time, they had travelled several miles along Route 1 and the traffic started getting heavy as they were now inside the town of Monterey.

"Let us take a detour and travel along the seventeen mile road and stop near the shore line where we can relax on the rocks," Johan suggested as he saw a sign that pointed in the direction of seventeen mile scenic road.

Kaya agreed as she was in a mood to see the ocean as well. They travelled for another ten minutes and entered the scenic route which was packed with many tourists in their cars who had come to enjoy the beautiful day. They had driven for another fifteen minutes when they came near a parking area, and Johan turned his car into the lot and parked. They both started walking towards the large stones near the sea shore and sat side by side on one of them holding hands. They sat motionless for several minutes not saying anything to one another.

All of a sudden, the sea breeze became intense and the waves turned ferocious, which was unusual for November. That did not bother either Johan or Kaya as they relaxed on the stone enjoying the huge waves as they slammed on the shore with intense force.

Then they heard a familiar sound coming from a not so great distance, a distinct sound of humpback whales.

"I love the sound of whales," Kaya observed.

"It seems like there is a family of whales; I hear both adult and baby whale sounds," added Johan. He was surprised at his own yogic power which had suddenly made him an expert on whale sounds. He quickly realized that he was no longer an ordinary human; he was only beginning to understand the true extent of many of the yogic powers he had mastered. The sounds became more frequent, and he could now sense that one of the adult whale voices was in agony. This sent a sudden chill through his body.

At that time, the unthinkable happened; Johan's body stiffened as he froze motionless, and he immediately collapsed without any warning, startling Kaya. Shocked, Kaya checked for his pulse, and his breathing which both seemed to be in order. She tried to force his eyelids to open which frightened her as she saw no life in those eyes.

What ensued over the next thirty minutes was utter panic for Kaya as she did not know how to respond; she simply stood up and waved for help as she was extremely nervous and could barely raise her voice to call out for help. Fortunately for her, one of the runners nearby saw her predicament, rushed to her, and promptly sat next to Johan and started checking his vital signs as Kaya stood next to him engulfed in fear and anxiety. It turned out that the man was a local doctor named Dr. Patterson. He assured Kaya that Johan was alright, and his initial thoughts were that Johan was probably in a mild coma. He, however, was puzzled that Johan had entered an instantaneous comatose without any signs of trauma or injury, and suggested that immediate medical attention was required to prevent any further complications. He promptly took out his phone and called for an ambulance from a nearby hospital.

"We need to take your friend to the hospital and do some CAT scans and MRI tests. It is impossible to say what is going on at this stage although all his vital signs are very normal," explained the doctor. They both then waited for the ambulance which came in less than fifteen minutes. However, this seemed like an eternity to Kaya.

"I will go with the ambulance, and you can follow us. Be brave and be assured that we will get to the bottom of this," suggested the doctor as the ambulance approached them.

Kaya reached the hospital, parked the car, and rushed into the hospital when a nurse approached her and asked her to fill out some forms for Johan. After the forms were filled out, the nurse suggested that she should wait for the doctors on the second floor.

The waiting room was dimly lit, and she realized that she was the only one in the room. As she sat waiting for the doctors to come out and tell her about Johan's health, she exchanged a series of texts with both Nick and PK, asking them to come and join her.

As she settled down in the waiting room, Kaya was overcome with uncontrollable emotions and she started sobbing quietly. The whole day had been too much for her to handle, and it had taken an unbelievable emotional toll on her. Tired, frustrated, and not sure what else to do, she slowly fell asleep in the chair. After a while, she heard some distant voices like they were coming from a faraway place which woke her from her sleep. As she tried to focus her eyes, she saw Dr. Patterson walking towards her with another doctor.

"This is Dr. Katz; he is a neurosurgeon who is attending to Johan" Dr. Patterson introduced the other doctor.

"We did a series of tests on Johan including MRI and CAT scan. We have not seen any physical trauma in the brain nor have we noticed anything unusual in his body. Moreover, all his vital signs are very normal and even his pupil size is normal, which is all very puzzling to us," narrated Dr. Katz in a business like fashion.

"Is he going to be alright, Doctor? Please tell me he is okay and that is all I want to know." Kaya sounded desperate as she wanted to get to the bottom of their assessment; any more delay would have broken her down.

"Of course. I expect him to recover within 48 hours. Nothing to worry about; I was just saying that I have never come across a case like this."

Kaya felt a little reassured and wanted to see Johan; she could no longer tolerate being separated from him.

"Can I see him?" she quizzed.

"Of course, let us walk to his room," suggested Dr. Katz.

Inside the private room, Johan was on a bed with several instruments monitoring his vital signs along with an IV feed. There was also a nurse who was writing down the readings from the instruments onto a chart every few minutes.

Kaya sat on the chair that was next to the bed and held Johan's hand staring at his face intently trying to silently communicate to him when she was distracted by Dr. Patterson's voice.

"Do you have any more questions?" asked Dr. Patterson. Kaya did not have any medical questions as the only thing that was on her mind was being close to Johan.

"How long can I stay here?"

"Well you can stay here for a couple of hours until the visiting hours are over. The nurse will give you her phone number, and you can always call her back to check on his status," Dr. Katz explained.

Within a few minutes the two doctors and the nurse had left the room, and Kaya was all by herself with Johan. She decided to sit there and wait for Nick and PK to join her.

Something strange and unexplainable happened as Kaya sat there watching Johan; she was overcome by a sudden urge to hold both of his hands. It was as though someone was commanding her to do exactly that, and she felt pressured. The pressure intensified and what started out as a mild urge became an uncontrollable desire. She bent over and held both his palms and slowly brought his right palm close to his left palm, all the while being careful not to disturb the monitoring devices. Why she was doing she had no idea; she felt like a robot that had been programmed to do so. She then took his right index finger and started making circles on his left palm, forming three such circles. Within seconds this desire stopped like a switch was being turned off and she realized that she was perspiring intensely.

She could not find an explanation for her strange behavior and wondered if it had some yogic significance. She knew that although Johan was in a coma, his yogic powers were still potent. She slowly positioned Johan's arms back to their original positions.

Just then she noticed some movements near the door and realized that Nick and PK had entered the room with the nurse. The moment she saw them, all her emotions came gushing back, and she hugged them together and started sobbing as the nurse left the room.

Over the next ten minutes, she had explained all that had happened beginning with everything Johan had narrated and closing with what Dr. Katz had told her.

"Don't worry, Kaya. He will be all right soon. We will take you back to your room and come back tomorrow. Hopefully he will be back to normal by then," assured PK.

Kaya knew that she could not stay here forever; she had to go back to her place, and this seemed like a good suggestion to her.

The nurse had now come back to the room to inform them that visiting hours were almost over.

"That is where all his stuff is placed, including his clothes and wallet. If there is anything else you want to keep there, let me know," explained the nurse as she pointed Kaya to a small closet at the corner of the room. Kaya took out the car keys and placed them in the closet next to his wallet, not knowing if it was a smart thing to do.

"Everything is safe here. No one is going to steal his personal belongings," assured the nurse, seeing Kaya's anxious look.

Kaya, Nick, and PK went back to the Bay area hoping to hear the good news about Johan soon. However, Dr. Katz was wrong, and Johan did not come out of coma in two days as he had predicted. Indeed, two weeks passed and Johan had shown no signs of coming out of his coma. Nor had his condition deteriorated; he continued to show normal vital signs which was all the more puzzling to Dr. Katz. During those two weeks, Kaya had made several trips to the hospital, and she was in continuous touch with the nurse about Johan's situation.

Exactly two weeks after Johan had been admitted to the hospital, something mysterious happened. It was very early in the morning, around 2 am, and a strange bird came down from the ocean side towards the hospital court yard. The bird was none other than Mitra. He hid himself in a tree nearby and waited for an opportune time to enter the building. His wait finally paid off when he saw a woman coming out of the lobby when the double door spread open. He immediately darted down at such an astonishing speed that the woman had no idea that a bird had flown by her and went inside the lobby. He then carefully hopped towards the stairs and went to the second floor without making any noise and soon he was inside Johan's room. Mitra was not alone; he was with Agni who had been sent by the yogi to bring Johan's body back to the Himalayas. Of course, finding Johan's soul was altogether a different problem.

Mitra stood still near Johan's body to make sure that Agni had transferred to Johan's body. Once his mission was completed, he slowly went to the semi-lit corridor and carefully went down the stairs waiting for the next opportunity for the automatic doors to open.

Once Agni was inside Johan's body, he slowly opened his eyes to get acclimated to the surroundings. He started accessing Johan's memory to ensure that he could perform the basic things that were required like driving and finding Johan's place. It took him around ten minutes to get hold of these memories, and once he had mastered it, he looked around to see how he could get out of that room. Luckily for Agni, all the monitoring devices had been removed as the doctors were convinced that there was no issue with Johan's vital signs. The only thing attached to the body was the IV line which he carefully removed. He then walked towards the closet and soon he was out of his robes and was clad in the old clothes. He put on his shoes and belt, grabbed his keys and very carefully walked towards the stairs. When the desk clerk was not attentive, he slipped out of the lobby and walked towards the car.

Within minutes, Agni was driving Johan's car towards the Bay area. Once he was inside the apartment, he went straight to the bedroom and picked up the backpack that had Johan's passport. After making sure that the visa to India was still valid, he went back to the car and started driving towards San Francisco International Airport. He wanted to be out of America as soon as possible and was ready to catch the next available flight to India on his way to his yogic master.

Epilogue

I have not heard back from Johan since Agni went back to India taking Johan's body with him. I assumed that he had reached the Himalayas safely and Johan's body was now secure in the cave next to the great yogi at the top of the Himalayas. Having been unwittingly brought into this mysterious yet unfolding story, I have been very curious as to what happened next. While the story that Johan narrated to me so far has been fantastic and fascinating, there were still myriads of unanswered questions as to what happened to Johan next – what happened to Johan's soul? Was the great yogi able to find Johan's lost soul and reunite it with his body?

I was also concerned about Kaya and wondered about the emotional toll that Johan's disappearance would have on her. My sincere hope was that Johan would come back, literally in one piece, body and soul together, so that she would finally able to reunite with Johan.

Even more intriguing was the next mission the yogi had in mind for Johan which he had mentioned subtly to Johan during the yogic lessons. I knew it was of utmost importance to the yogi as he had trained and helped Johan acquire all those yogic powers specifically for that mission. I was also curious about the meaning of all those visions Johan had as a child, especially the towering inferno. Did it have a spiritual significance or did it have something to do with Johan's past life?

Above all, the yogi himself was an enigma to me as there were so many mysteries surrounding him. There were endless questions in my mind about the yogi's past. What were his origins? How had he become a yogi? And my questions did not end there either.

It was painfully clear to me that none of the questions could be answered by anyone, not even by Nick or Kaya, even if I were lucky enough to track them. The only option for me was to wait for the call from Johan. Needless to say, I am still waiting for that call from him although I am very much aware that the moment he tries to reach me, I would have a severe migraine headache. After all, it is not going to be a simple wireless call or a text message! Meanwhile, I sit and wait for that call in Plano, Texas so that I can chronicle the next phase of Johan's adventure.

Also by Dr. Mysore N. Prakash

The Courtesan and the Sadhu
A Novel about Maya, Dharma, and God

Synopsis

This novel is set in ancient India just after Alexander the Great's invasion, taking the reader through the spiritual journey of two seekers. Kautilya, the first seeker, is a Vedic scholar very close to finding The Truth. However, his life takes an unexpected detour, and he ends up building the Mauryan Empire. Although successful in re-establishing dharmic values in the Indian sub-continent, and getting rid of the vestiges of Alexander's invasion, he continues to have inner struggles about the path he has chosen. Manu, the other seeker, is an elite warrior in the Mauryan Army but ends up becoming a seeker of Truth at a young age. Disappointed in love, he tries to find answers to his spiritual questions, first as a Buddhist monk and later as a Sadhu. In this story, the author takes the reader through the intriguing journey of the two seekers as they finally overcome Maya to reach Moksha (emancipation), but was it the path specified by The Enlightened One or was it God Himself?

This is a novel about Empire-building and God Consciousness with a love story intertwined between the two.

Reviews

"This is a fascinating story set in ancient India, conveying timeless truths that speak to readers from all cultures of our twenty-first century world. A delightful read indeed! All in all, this is an excellent, moving, and religiously inspiring work that deserves wide readership. "

> *— Ruben L.F. Habito, Professor of World Religions and Spirituality, Southern Methodist University, Dallas, Texas.*

"This book takes the reader on an epic spiritual journey while weaving together several of the major religious traditions of India. The novel presents a compelling tale of vivid characters interacting across both time and geography. Set in Ancient India, the novel combines all of the requisites of good story-telling: adventure, romance, and a variety of lessons for achieving a happier existence. The book is accessible to readers of all levels and serves as a lively cultural introduction to South Asia. A delight for the reader who is seeking something both different and substantive."

> *— Robert C. Wigton, J.D., Ph.D., Professor of Political Science, Eckard College, St. Petersburg, Florida*